P9-DUZ-427

The Wind

WITHDRAWN
UTSA Libraries

The Wind

A Novella by Patricia Barone

— with Artworks by the Author —

Minnesota Voices Project Number 28

NEW RIVERS PRESS 1987

Copyright © 1987 by Patricia Barone
Library of Congress Catalog Card Number: 86-63554
ISBN: 0-89823-085-3
All rights reserved
Design and typesetting: Peregrine Publications, St. Paul

The Wind has been published with the aid of grants from the Jerome Foundation, the
Dayton Hudson Foundation (with funds provided by B. Dalton Bookseller), the First
Bank System Foundation, and the National Endowment for the Arts (with funds ap-
propriated by the Congress of the United States.

New Rivers Press books are distributed by:

The Talman Company	and	Bookslinger
150-5th Ave.		213 E. 4th St.
New York, NY 10011		St. Paul, MN 55101

The Wind has been manufactured in the United States of America for New Rivers
Press, Inc. (C. W. Truesdale, editor/publisher), 1602 Selby Ave., St. Paul, MN
55104 in a first edition of 1,500 copies.

LIBRARY
The University of Texas
At San Antonio

For Stan

and

My Mother and Father

*I would like to thank
Dr. Kathrin Asper and Ms. Diana Nowatzki, P.T.
for their loving and invaluable guidance
in the areas of psychology and physical therapy.*

*I would also like to thank my editor,
Roger Blakely, not only for his careful
attention to my work, but also for his
warm encouragement.*

Born of the wind, of the air, of lightning, of the light, may the shell born from gold . . . defend us from fear! . . . May the pearl protect thee!

A hymn of the Ahtarva Vada

Part One

The Wind

The wind was at her back. But it seemed to collect in pockets at the four corners of the large painting she carried. So that, walking across the Washington Avenue Bridge, Fran twisted and turned. Below, on either side of the Mississippi, cars pulsed like mechanical insects. Wind-up toys along a painted stream. And all so easy to glide. She thought of the beginning of a friend's poem.

> A bird drawn down:
> power
> in the water.

Was she getting to be one of those people who were attracted to heights? The thought formed: *If I were to put both hands on the painting and raise it above my head . . .*

1

ALAN WAS WAITING FOR HER when she got in at almost midnight.
"Smell that?" he called from the kitchen, "I've got something to make
you forget how tired you are!"

"Be with you in a minute." She dropped her heavy canvas sack of
turpentine, oil and brushes and ran for the bathroom. Something had
happened at work? At the U.? He had a theory that people could be
classified by the way their bowels reacted to tension. Fran got the
runs; Alan himself became constipated.

He sat with his legs extended from their early Salvation Army
couch, which, except for one table, a lamp and four cushions, was
their only piece of livingroom furniture. Above it hung two O'Keefe
prints, each with an even film of dust, each fixed to the wall with con-
cealed masking-tape loops.

Fran had propped her painting against the wall that faced the windows: a long narrow panel of glass close to ceiling height, half-leaded
in a stylized flower pattern. Alan wasn't surprised that she wouldn't
hang her paintings in the dark. "Not for interior decoration,"
said Fran.

When she came back, she lowered herself onto the couch, her hand
against the small of her back. "Italian stuffed artichokes?"

"And claret."

"That's really . . . hey, you went to a lot of trouble. But do you
mind if I don't eat just yet? You go ahead."

Alan tore off a large leaf from the bottom. Crumbs of parmesan fell
onto his sweater. He took a swallow of his wine, and pretended
that he was thinking about the chess move he was working out from
Chess Moves of the Masters, the book she'd given him last Christmas.
He moved the board to one side of a warp in the veneer.

When he looked at her again, she had closed her eyes. Lately, she
seemed less sturdy, more pared down, her broad cheekbones exposed.
Women with narrow jaws and thin noses were too changeable. Yet,
in a year or so, perhaps, she'd show the hairline wrinkles of a fair
skinned woman, cracks in the glaze, a subtle erosion. Hard to believe
that age would come to Fran. She was too damn stubborn. Yet, if Fran
would only change, not age . . . enough of that.

She opened her eyes. "God, it's annoying to have you look at me
when my eyes are closed. I can feel you staring." But then she smiled,
and said, "That looks good," and picked off an artichoke leaf, begin-

ning at the top as she always did. Then she'd switch to the bottom, or either side. She had no regard for the intricate, ordered spiral an artichoke makes, but tossed her eaten leaves any which way on the morning's sports page. Not what you'd expect from an artist. He laid his eaten leaves, one by one, in a cupped circle around his plate.

He gave her ten minutes, then he said, "About my suggestion this afternoon . . ."

"You mean about painting at home? I quit my job at the hospital?"

"Fran. I mean an inside job. Why don't you want to have a baby? We can't wait much longer with you almost 33." There. He'd said it, and couldn't have made a worse job of it. All that planning only to get her back up.

After she stomped into the kitchen, Alan rose heavily, piled several dirty dishes, cups and glasses — most of them Fran's — on a stack of newspapers, then almost collided with her as she came back through the door with a glass of mineral water. He didn't comment on the load he carried. What would be the use? Once she told him that doing repeatable tasks made her feel guilty about wasting time.

Looking more thoughtful than annoyed, she turned the painting she'd put against the wall when she came home. So he tried again, from another angle. "You could use the time home with a baby to work on your masters at the U."

She stuck both hands in her pockets and rocked back and forward on her heels. "That's out now. You just assumed there'd be no problem with my acceptance, and so did I. Vincent said I should stick around next year, take some courses. Let the department get familiar with my work. Which meant they aren't admitting me to the grad program next fall. I was so mad that I told him their graduate painting department exhibit was too bad to hang. He asked why, then, did I want to be admitted? Good question!"

"It's all politics over there," he said. "You told me yourself it's incestuous. He probably wanted to sign you up for the Los Angeles summer school trip he leads. Give him a sign, and then don't come across."

"Always the angles, Alan. I'm really mad. It's humiliating to be turned down for a place in a mediocre program. It was a try for a degree and a better paying job. I'd be happier just painting and getting advice from people I could respect, like Liz and Steve."

She moved the painting slightly , so that the floor lamp was directly overhead. "This is the best thing I've done," she said. "Vincent is an ass."

Alan moved so that he too could look at it. He was amused because she really was thinking more about her composition than her rejection.

11

Fran specialized in flat surfaces. Hard-edged with just a blur behind — as if concealing another, more energetic plane pushing up. People would begin to pass one of her paintings, then they'd stop, backing up a little as if looking for an op-art trick: "What color is that? It changes!" Her grays turned red next to green — a hidden violence elicited by the viewer. Lately, even Fran herself has found it necessary to contain her work with the device of an all-over grid.

"You're absolutely right. You don't have to go to grad school to paint," he said, and then, "Things have changed now that I'm a regular stringer for *Omni* and the *Sunday Tribune*. I've been trying to tell you that we can afford for you to stay home. And now we won't have to worry about your tuition." Alan heard the words coming out of his mouth. What had he done! Pledged himself to do more features, declared his fealty to magazines and newspapers — that was what. He really wanted to write his own short stories, and maybe a novel some day . . . Even as he made his generous offer to Fran, he felt a familiar stab at the right side of his waist line. A pain that didn't really go away, but just went deeper, so that, when he was on vacation, he had to poke the spot with his finger to find it. Back in harness, when he had a deadline, it cramped spasmodically; spastic colon the doctor said, and nothing to worry about. But Alan looked upon the pain as his risk barometer. Freelancing was a risky business. The pain was often like the old stitch in time saves nine. But he couldn't take back what he'd said, just modify it. "I *think* we can afford it for a year."

"But you've put more than a financial condition on my staying home." She sat down and looked right into his eyes.

Alan felt encouraged. Although he knew it might be the wrong thing to say, he couldn't resist: "What you really want is . . . "

"Don't tell me what I really."

"You want a place to be safe, to create your own world. Like making tree houses, leaf pile mansions, and clay dugouts when you were ten." An intentional evocation. Was he being too obvious? He flicked his chess pieces into a circular barricade.

Fran had to smile, though sourly. "Privacy. It was emotional Monopoly: my Boardwalk Kingdom."

The direction of their conversation pleased him. But he just sat with her for a while because he saw that, once again, she wanted to look at her painting. Not the time for probing or analysis. A paradox, he thought: I'm still fascinated with her silences, and yet I'm always trying to get her to talk. All his writing friends with their over-easy words. Fran should be a relief.

He remembered the first time he saw her eyes shift from opacity, become transparent. An almost sexual entrance, and connected to a certain type of reminiscence, like the time she told about picking blueberries on Skabroud's sand spit. The slight dilation of her pupils, a shift in the spiky blue iris toward green.

So, Alan thought, in the eleven years of our marriage, we have, after all, developed a familiar mythological country. Although Fran was usually impatient with repetition, in their private country she agreed with him: "If a story is good the first time, it's good forever."

Early in their marriage, she'd told him a very interesting dream in which she was a small girl on a train with her parents, her brothers and sisters, and her elderly aunts and uncles. It seemed that the train wasn't stopping where it should. Alan, who was waiting for her, would be left at some unnamed station. The train arrived and no one got off but the old people and Frances. Aunt Claire tried to console her. There were giant sunflowers, but they all turned their heads away. She was inordinately upset about this dream, which came just a few days before she had a miscarriage — so early she hadn't known for sure that she was pregnant.

Now she sat cross-legged on the sofa studying her painting. Her artichoke lay ravaged on the coffee table, as if a mouse had gnawed it. Alan had also left his, half-eaten, on his plate.

Always before, they had eaten their artichokes slowly, sipping wine. After seeing the movie "10", Alan started putting Ravel's Bolero on the stereo and they'd eat more purposefully, excising the purple choke hairs, and come to their hearts together. He plucked a leaf, chewed slowly. The stuffing had too much olive oil this time. He said, impatiently, "Let's try to make some order out of all this. It's like a chess game in a way. Why don't you pick up your Rook? It's fate. Unconsciously, you fixed the game so you wouldn't have to go to graduate school." He waved the King. "Like castling."

"I haven't had a period for two months."

Pulling an artichoke leaf down his front teeth, he almost gagged on the meat he nipped from the bottom. "I don't know what to say!" More peevish than surprised, so Fran laughed. His chuckle turned to a genuine guffaw, which stopped abruptly when she put her face in her hands. "Fran, they say there are fewer accidents than people think."

"This wasn't an accident. I threw away the diaphragm three months ago."

"I don't understand. I thought you didn't . . . "

"I'm really scared, but I've gotten so tired of being undecided."

He lifted his glass in slow motion. And, after a fraction of a second, she did too. This gave him permission to celebrate.

2

THE NEXT MORNING Fran decided she'd better get something else over with. Her graduate portfolio was still at the University of Minnesota. It was no small matter to transport, because some of her paintings were twelve square feet in area. Tying seven canvases to the luggage rack of a Volkswagon didn't seem like a good idea. But their friend with a van had gone to Bemidji.

They'd just crossed the Mississippi over the Washington Avenue bridge when one of the paintings edged, corner down, onto the windshield.

"God, pull over, Alan, quick!"

He did, but too late. Their speed had given lift, so all her kites took wind — blown toward traffic, unrelenting metal: the work of three years gone. He pulled over to the shoulder, put his emergency lights on, while she threw open the door of their car. Only his shout, "Fran, are you crazy!" and his hand on the back of her collar, kept her inside, kept her from stopping cars and trucks — with her body? "Your life — it's not worth your life!" So she screamed and though she couldn't wrench free of Alan's grip, she saw herself die, saw her bones break, blow to either side of the highway. Then, "All is not lost!" Alan said. Was . . . some of her canvas skin saved? It took just minutes to salvage the wreckage of five paintings. Deboned, the deflated canvases fit inside. The survivor went home, and was sick to know: What she made was Frances.

Alan fixed tea for them. She felt grateful for his silence. After a while, she got up, went to her studio and came back with stretchers, a pliers, and a staple gun. "Mind if I work in here with you?" She restretched the canvases, which took all afternoon. "The surfaces are damaged, but I think I won't mind working on them again." Then, a little later: "Maybe these weren't finished after all." She tried to remember the two missing canvases, but lying in oily tatters on the highway, they refused to rise up whole. What was gone was gone. The lost canvases were finished. It was already dark when she looked at the remaining five and said, "Maybe there will be some changes."

On Sunday she was still brooding. "Alan, the wind was so strange on Friday after my interview. It reminded me of something . . . I feel awful, like I'd almost died because I was hysterical about losing my paintings. You could have been killed trying to stop me."

"I was afraid you'd run in front of a semi. It was also my fault. I should have realized we couldn't transport your paintings on our car."

"Alan, that's right! You aren't really connected to my paintings." Her voice sounded sharp, even to herself. "But it was my own fault. I shouldn't expect you to take better care of my work than I do myself. It's wrong not to care for yourself."

She got up for yet another cup of camomile tea; the warmth comforted her hands. "The wind on Friday reminded me of the fall after my little brother drowned. One day I crossed Olson Avenue to play in the Altesheimer apple orchard, and I climbed to the top of the tallest tree. The wind made the tree alive — like an animal trying to toss me out. I half enjoyed being afraid. Then my mother screamed my name — right out of the wind. She pulled me down from the tree and scolded me all the way home. It was the first time I realized that grownups got scared too. You see, Michael had crossed that same street on his way to the parkway creek."

She saw, too late, that Alan was getting intense. At times like this his brown eyes looked black. "Fran, I've often wondered why you never said much about his death. Why didn't you ever tell me about your mother coming to find you? The way you talked — it's like it happened yesterday."

She might have known he'd be too interested. She'd wanted to say something, she'd said it, and now why dwell on it? "What good does it do to talk about something like that? It's over." Picking up two of her paintings by the stretchers, she turned toward her studio in a back bedroom, so quickly she almost tripped on a loose thread from the canvas. She smiled at him, to soften her exit. "Can I bring you back a glass of wine?"

They were passing the weekend, Fran thought, in siege. Gentle. A Mozart flute concerto on MPR. Reading the *Sunday Tribune* together. She trailed her fingers across his back each time she passed his chair. An undercurrent of anger towards him. Unreasonable.

Alan asked, "How do you feel?" And Fran suspected he was really asking about the baby. But neither of them had to talk about it yet. The baby could live for a while yet in a fictional country of its own.

15

3

BY THE TIME FRAN ARRIVED at St. Clothilde's, the day shift had already left. The head nurse looked at her watch. "Sorry," Fran told her as she went to the assignment board for her work sheet. Eight beds to straighten, one bath left over, one post-op, dinner trays at five. Good, Katherine Morgan on her list. Katherine, who seemed too young, at 62, for this geriatric ward. If it's quiet later, maybe they'll have a chance to talk.

Fran did the tub bath first. On the day shift, she had to do eight baths, eight tub scrubs — her usual number of patients. She wondered why she didn't mind cleaning the bathrooms at the hospital. She could be alone with her thoughts — that was why, while her hands rubbed away layers of dry skin and calcium deposit.

While Fran was easing Mrs. Olafson into the tub, the old woman was incontinent. "Oh, oh, oh, how dreadful for you, Frances. I'm so embarrassed."

Fran thought to say, "But you couldn't help it!" then didn't. That was exactly what troubled Mrs. Olafson. It would be easier if she were also senile. Instead Fran said, "Honestly, I don't mind."

While cleaning the tub again, she was reminded, sharply, and all at once, of her grandmother. Sweetpeas and lavander sachet — that was Grandma too. Odd. Now why would cleaning a bathroom . . . The odor of Ajax and diarrhea. Grandma living alone at 87, out of choice, and despite a prolapsed bowel.

Fran recalled the time, sixteen years ago, when she and her mother visited Grandma and found her watching her soap serials, while sitting on newspapers to protect the brocade of the parlor sofa.

"It's nothing! A nuisance, nothing more," Grandma said. But she only protested a little. Then she was persuaded to go home with them, where she died within a year of heart failure.

Fran though about how, when she'd left the old house for the last time, she felt an admiration for the way her grandmother worked, and kept her environment clean (an odor of Ajax and diarrhea). Fran knew then that coming to live with them would be her grandmother's loss.

***

When Fran brought in her dinner tray, Katherine looked up and smiled. "How nice. Even lukewarm swiss steak is a welcome interruption." She pointed to the minutes of her professional association, *The Psychologists' Forum* (held before her on a wire holder attached to the swing tray). "I've lost the edge, Fran. Either this stroke took more brain cells than I thought, or this stuff has been gobbledlygook all the time and I didn't know it." Around the hospital they referred to Katherine as one of the "cerebrovascular accidents." But it was hard to remember her partial paralysis when she spoke. The stroke might have been an accident — she was not an accident.

Absently, Fran leaned over and put her hand on the bow of Katherine's wire rim spectacles, which caught the evening sun with every dust spot and spatter. "Katherine, can I clean your glasses?"

Katherine laughed — a strangled low snorting. "I don't think that will help my eyesight all that much, but thank you!"

Fran felt herself flushing, though she knew Katherine wasn't laughing at *her*. "Sister Helen told the aides that she had a test for the quality of patient care: How clean did we keep their eyeglasses?" Fran wiped the lenses carefully on a flannel sheet, then raised the back of the bed, and adjusted the bedside table for the tray. "I bet any reading loss is only temporary—nothing to do with your . . . mind. You make a lot more sense to me than most people who haven't had strokes. What I mean to say, is . . . sometimes, I don't use words well . . ."

"You didn't almost lose your words. I'm glad lightning struck on the right side."

"I have to run now. I'll bring your Postum at ten."

Later that evening, when Katherine again saw her from her stricken side, almost as soon as she entered the room, Fran decided there really had been an improvement in the past month, and felt grateful, in a confused way, relieved. Faces first, and then print. Wasn't that what the therapist said? Soon she'll have less trouble with those professional journals. Yet there was something else in her feeling. It's that she wanted Katherine to be stronger for her, for Fran. She wanted something from her.

They sat together in silence for a few moments. Then Fran said, "Alan thinks it's a good thing that graduate school fell through. He says that now I can stay home and paint and have a baby."

"What do you want to do?"

"I want to stay home and paint. The baby I'm not so sure of. How did therapy go today?"

"She's got me on my hands and knees. Maybe next week I'll be kneeling." Katherine smiled. "Gotta crawl before you can walk!"

Fran asked, diffidently, "Do you get discouraged, having to start all over again like an infant? Do you sometimes want to just get up between those parallel bars and force yourself to walk?"

"Good question. No . . . no, I'm right where I should be. I'd have to be angry with my body to try to force it. Slow and easy and I'll get there."

4

FRAN HOOKED HER ARM under Katherine's arm, put her shoulder into the lift, and eased her big-boned body into the wheelchair.

"I'm not too heavy for you?"

"You mean because of my . . . Alan already asked Dr. Marcus. I have to avoid lifting my own weight, so to speak. You pivot yourself on your good leg, so there's not that much weight for me."

Katherine picked at the nap of the blanket Fran used to cover her knees. "Well, then listen. I've been thinking about the future, and that's hard to do in this place." She looked out the door of her room, and Fran followed her gaze, hearing, as if for the first time, the layers of sound that made up a day on the ward: the clatter of a meals cart rounding the corner, the squeaking of a gurney, the insistent monotony of the PA voice. And none of the noise, for a moment, seemed connected to a source; the aides, orderlies, and nurses moved up and down the corridor, in and out of rooms as if projected — a foreign film with the sound superimposed and a little bit off . . .

"About the future," Katherine said again, and looked at Fran. "Doesn't the mix of smells bother you now?"

"You mean because of . . . no. Well, yes in a way." But, her stomach, she felt sure, would inevitably learn to cope with the various antiseptics, alcohol smells that assaulted the lining of her nose and plummeted — giving her diaphragm a jolt, but it passed, and she'd get used to urine or even vomit. Despite a queasy first trimester, she hadn't allowed herself to be sick. But would she ever be able to care for Mrs. Ohm again, without ducking out the door every few minutes to breathe in the hall away from the dead-sweet odor of cancer?

"Fran, I have a proposal for you, for Alan too, I guess. What would you think of taking a job with me, doing the sorts of things you do here as a nursing assistant, and some housekeeping, so I can go back into practice? In two months, the therapist says I should be able to stand by myself and walk a few steps." Katherine took a deep breath, and waited, but Fran only nodded, not yes, but telling her to continue. "As an out-patient, I'll continue with therapy here, and you'll have to take me for an hour each afternoon." She looked at Fran again, and Fran thought: Could I have a schedule — something to replace knowing what should happen — even if it doesn't — for eight hours each day. I would miss putting my feet on automatic pilot, miss taking around the water at ten while my mind's in a painting . . .

"I plan to buy the duplex adjoining mine. My half would now be both living quarters and office. You and Alan and the baby would have enough privacy on your side, except that I would feel more secure if we could have an intercom. Well, say something."

Katherine looked at once so fidgety and thwarted by her semi-paralysis that Fran flushed and took her patient's hands. How locked-in they *both* were. And she had to be reminded to speak. Dropping her hands, she said, "I'll have to talk this over with Alan." She wanted to say yes and then wanted to say no. Why did people insist on complicating things? "Thank you, Katherine, thank you. I'll let you know after I talk to Alan. I think we should take at least a week to think about it."

Recently Alan had said, "Katherine this, Katherine that. You make her out to be a cross between Eleanor Roosevelt and Emma Jung. What has impresed you so about her?" His question made Fran realize how little she knew about Katherine. Once again she was having difficulty explaining a feeling to Alan. Because he seemed to want credentials or something — facts. Fran told him that Katherine lived alone. "Well," Alan said, and waited. Living alone had a weight for her that Alan didn't understand. Katherine had been a widow for ten years and she didn't have any children. Her sister Peggy had married a Swiss and lived in Zurich. She had colleagues and one or two close women friends. That was all. The uncluttered life, Fran thought, and realized that she approved and identified with Katherine's limited connections. And to think of how often she had chimed in with the others saying what a shame that Mrs. so-and-so had so few visitors.

"Well, Fran, I can't know what you find to talk about."

Now that Katherine's offer had caused a silence to fall between them, Fran was glad to push Katherine's wheelchair onto the elevator for physical therapy. She remembered when she first wanted to get to know Katherine. It was the day that she overheard her conversation with Miss Bundy and Mrs. Jensen in the patient's lounge. Miss Bundy was on her usual riff, as Alan would say, about her sister and nieces never coming to see her. The ward staff no longer paid much attention to the woman's complaints, because nothing anyone did or said seemed to comfort her. So Fran was surprised when Katherine said something that stopped the flow. A long silence, and Fran moved closer so that she could hear better. Miss Bundy said, "I'm glad you asked me that. Yes, my sister Annie was only about five — it was before she started school — when Grandma died, and she remembers how Grandma used to sit in a sort of courtyard in the old house, before they added on and made a dining room between the kitchen and the parlor, and she made butter, with a long thin rectangular churn. Annie is like Gran. She's older than me, but she's so strong that she won't leave the family home till a tornado blows the roof off like that one in 1908 did Gran's. And here I am at only seventy-five."

"And here I am at sixty-two," said Katherine. "It's very hard."

Fran told Alan how Miss Bundy patted Katherine's hand, and assured her she'd better. Miss Bundy's voice sounded stronger than it had in months.

Alan seemed very interested in just how Katherine changed Miss Bundy's attitude: It didn't seem to be much that she *said* because she said so little. He asked Fran a lot of questions, and Fran felt like telling him not to put her friend in one of his stories, but didn't. She liked Alan's stories, but hated the thought that he drew upon their common life to write them.

Katherine may have changed Miss Bundy's attitude, but Fran wondered if Katherine herself were changed — from the time before the stroke when Fran hadn't known her. Strokes changed people's personalities. They saw it all the time on the ward. Marge Dickson had been a lawyer, her niece said, and quite satisfied living alone with her absorbing case load and "only one stiff whiskey after work, thank you." But now she wanted her family to do everything for her but shit, said her niece and what a shame because the therapist thought she could have been fairly independent if she had only wanted to work at getting better. How much had Katherine's stroke changed her? Before her stroke did she become so immersed in what people were telling her that she tapped her index finger on her teeth and didn't realize it? Not the worst habit — not like picking your nose. But it seemed odd for a psychologist to be, what did they call it — unconscious, or at least unselfconscious. But Katherine was never out-of-it. Certainly not like Tillie Napsen, who was apt to make devastating remarks to staff and visitors alike: Last week she'd said one of the aides looked just like that tramp her Herb went off with after the war.

"So what do you talk about?" said Alan. Fran thought, oh — he's thinking about us again. He's jealous. But she only said, "Just yesterday, knowing she had an interest in dreams, I told her one I had: I was crossing a bridge and there was a sudden wind of almost hurricane force. I got down on my hands and knees and began to crawl. I found that I had to grab at the iron bars of the railing to keep from being blown away. A young couple, who were also crossing the bridge, were trying to remain upright. Somehow I felt responsible for their safety, though I knew if I kept on crawling, I'd reach the other side. I wonder why my paintings weren't in the dream — it was like crossing the bridge the day before that bad experience on the freeway."

"Why didn't you tell me that one before?"

21

"Well, now I have."

"That's probably a pregnancy dream, let me check it out . . . "
Alan said, as he half rose from his chair.

"Must you get your dream interpretation book, Alan?"

"Oh, why not — you don't have to believe it; think of it as fun to think about."

While he rummaged in his bookcase and the four boxes he kept in the closet, Fran thought that she had plenty to think about already — and none of it fun. Yes, Katherine's offer was a real problem-solver, the problem being her own pregnancy as much as Katherine's disability. But what about after pregnancy? If she stayed home because of Katherine it meant she'd have to stay home with the baby too. She'd been fantasizing about another scenario: a competent older woman who would take care of the baby for her when she — admit it! — *fled* to an outside job. But if she did that, she'd also be fleeing from her painting. She might be having pregnancy dreams, but this was certainly not a dream pregnancy.

Alan came back with his fingers in two books. "The dream covers more ground than I thought. I think I'm in it too. But before I tell you what I've found, what do *you* think it means?"

"I don't know."

"I think it has something to do with almost losing your paintings like you said and with the danger we were in. But I think it's mostly about your pregnancy."

"Alan, this isn't the sort of dream I feel like diagramming. As a matter of fact, I remember now that my mother had sent me to the dentist."

"A classic textbook illustration of a pregnancy dream."

5

*F*RAN BEGAN THINKING OF HER PAST, as if pulling old photographs out of a desk drawer. Like a developing polaroid snapshot, people emerged from a gray receding mist, and were gradually, one leg at a time, embodied. She brought forth an image of her parents' 35th wedding anniversary: Her five brothers and sisters and their wives, husbands and a few children around "grandma," and "grandpa." On dark days it seemed that Michael was a double-exposure, a ghost-image in that photo, forever young-dead, younger than the oldest grandchild. When people asked about her family, she sometimes said that she was the first of seven. But other times she said she was the eldest of six — when she was feeling most settled into her daily routine, and her work was going well, when she thought only of her life the way it turned out to be — as shown in any print, the negatives safely forgotten in the bottom drawer. She couldn't locate what she most clearly remembered in the anniversary print of the family, her parents (See — they survived!), only an approximation. Fran, who never carried photographs in her wallet, had brought a picture to show Katherine. In tones of sepia and peach, it was —

"After the renewal of vows, outside the church, we spoke of the sunset and then threw rice."

Katherine murmured, "Time-markings."

Fran continued, "In the family, when someone leaves, we stand along the road with our hands behind our backs until the last minute when we wave dishcloths, even sheets, thought it's hard to hide a sheet."

"Leave-takings," said Katherine. She took the damp wash cloth from Fran with her right hand.

Fran gently massaged the bent fingers of the left hand, while she continued reminiscing. "My grandfather used to say, 'Well, don't stand in the doorway all night. If you're going to be going, then go.' This has become a family saying, my mother's really. She is very matter-of-fact, very directive. Yet she doesn't try to hold onto people in any obvious way."

When Katherine asked Fran what she meant, at first Fran didn't know what to say. What she had told Katherine was a contradiction. *How* did her mother try to hold onto her children, when she constantly urged their strength and independence? "She's like . . . the morning coffee she makes, with lots of milk and sugar, but too strong. She's macho. For example — My sister Cress, who lives in Duluth, went to stay with my parents in Minneapolis so Mom could help her convalesce after she lost a baby in her eighth month, and she spent most of one week crying at our parents' kitchen table — who could blame her — while her husband stayed with their six year old. I'd come over for a day, and was just about to leave, when my mother said, 'All right, Cress, you can't go on like this. There's no use crying about something you can't do anything about. Your husband needs you, and most of all, that little boy needs you.' Then Mom brought out a bottle of brandy and poured some in a glass and handed it to Cress, who is a big coffee drinker. Mom said, 'Now drink this slowly, and notice how you begin to feel — soon, a bit unreal, because your nerves will be soothed. But because your baby is gone, when you feel better, even if it's purely physical, you might feel guilty. But don't! Unless living itself is a guilty act, and it isn't. You only have cause to feel wrong if you *don't* live!"

"What did your sister do?"

"She drank it."

"I hope she didn't get into the habit."

"You think that my mother was . . . inappropriate?" Fran regretted telling Katherine about her mother and Cress, and was also feeling a little — soiled, which came from talking too much.

"Oh, Fran, how insensitive of me! I didn't really mean anything of the sort. I just spoke without thinking, without thinking about what your mother's attitude could have meant for your sister. It was probably a very good thing to say — in effect, she wasn't just telling your sister to pull herself together — which, all alone, would have been a bit unfeeling, but was also telling her to accept comfort. I admit I have a little trouble with that *form* of comfort." Katherine peered at her, leaned forward a little, and, because she was frowning out of her still-semi-frozen face, she looked lopsided, even comical.

Fran stopped feeling angry with Katherine and said, "Well, I think the way my mom treated Cress was . . effective, but still too tough. I think my mother was armored for life by her perfect childhood, so she doesn't understand people grieving, and certainly not people who are weak."

"Or maybe not so constitutionally optimistic?"

"Yes . . . But you can be born with a happy or contented temperament, and then have it spoiled for you by bad luck, bad providence. Think of all the people who would be happy as could be just doing their own work, if they were only left alone . . . " Fran felt as if she were babbling. And the water was getting cold. Time to turn the subject away from her family! "What about you, Katherine," she said, "it must have been very difficult to lose . . . " But she felt all at once embarrassed — for talking about herself so much before and for seeming to pry. Katherine was as old as her mother . . .

But Katherine only said, quickly, "Thank you dear. It took me a long time to get over losing my husband."

Fran felt relieved. Maybe Katherine would *like* to talk more about her life? "And it must have been hard for you and your sister when your parents died."

"My sister? Oh — you mean Peggy. My — our — parents died almost forty years ago now. I was still in graduate school." Katherine managed to turn, with minimal assistance, onto her side. "Mind you do a good job with me, Fran. Mrs. Adams was taken away for her funeral after her bed bath yesterday."

"Most of the work is yours today." Fran was supposed to encourage the stroke patients to do as much for themselves as possible. Sweat beads formed on Katherine's forehead from the effort it took to raise her left arm, straight-elbowed, only forty-five degrees from her lap. Fran eased on the sleeves of the bed jacket.

It was a minute before Katherine seemed to have the breath to talk. "Speaking of funerals and time-markings, when your Grandma died, the one who lived with you, did your mother have good neighbors? Did they bring over their best hot dish? When we don't know what to do for someone, we try to feed them. I've often thought it's like saying, 'You're going to live so you'll need this.' "

"Maybe my mother was saying that to Cress. I don't know. I don't remember much about my grandmother's funeral. But I remember everything about the day my brother died. Didn't I tell you my four year old brother drowned when I was eight?" She sounded disingenuous, even to herself. The pregnancy has caused her to think every day of her brother.

Katherine was looking at her, a question in her eyes, so Fran continued. "My mother said, 'Thank God I had the two of you left.' She went on to have four more."

"Wasn't it good she had faith in life?"

"Good? People do what they can do. I wouldn't give God another chance to decide if he'd let me keep a child. The more you have, the more you stand to lose." Fran wrung out the washcloth, and tossed it, along with the towel, into the hamper. She felt expectant, and consequently, her words sounded, in her own ears, a little too dramatic. But she also felt like snapping the towel, like kicking the hamper, and she was content in the thought that Katherine guessed how she felt.

25

6

KATHERINE WISHED SHE COULD lock her door. Pregnancy, a brother's death. That wasn't a casual conversation. There was another question, so far avoided — what of her own judgment? The exchange with Fran was too much like therapeutic listening. And she had blundered, been a little — though not with serious effect — unthinking.

And why hadn't she corrected that mistake? How had Peggy come, in the first place, to be listed as her "next of kin"? It must have been her incoherence after the stroke. When growing up, they were as close as sisters. It's funny how the stroke put her back fifty years ago! But, however understandable, an error was an error, she'd seen it on her records and she hadn't, yet, gotten around to setting the record straight . . . Fran was going to decide to come and live with her — she knew it. And she knew that now she'd never be able to tell the truth about Peggy. She *had* to have a "sister" in reserve. Then if it didn't work out with Fran, she had a prior life to return to! She would move to Zurich! One little lie, and she was protected from being a pitiable person with no family. On the contrary, she was a professional woman seeking to continue her professional life. Who was she trying to kid? Would she even be *able* to continue her practice? A feeling, as if struggling to the surface from a deep dive, when you run out of air. Then — up and out, with the sudden thought of Fran, that she might brood about revealing herself. Katherine decided to forget, for the time, about psychology. As a friend, she would ask Fran more about Michael.

And Fran seemed glad to talk. A picture of Michael's last summer, 28 years ago, formed in Katherine's mind:

The merry-go-round, childhood, spun out. Mike Malley was thrown off. But then the slow round began again, with every summer like every other summer but that one, and birthdays the same, then Christmas still smelling of crushed pine needles in the dark.

Katherine wondered how long it was before Fran no longer started, and squirmed when she recalled, not Michael, but her crime against Michael. "The day before he died," she said, "I hit him and really wanted to hurt him because he wanted some of my red paper. Afterwards, I thought, why didn't I give him just one piece!"

Fran told how she used to daydream about saving her brother. "I felt if only I had stayed home to watch him," she said, "he wouldn't have died!" Katherine thought, how easy it is for children to be overresponsible! How long was it before Fran returned to childhood?

If ever?

When Fran left, Katherine lay back on her bed and closed her eyes, which she did whenever a memory eluded her: an image of a crying small child held by another — Peggy in front of PS-22, holding her little sister after the school bus grazed her, knocked her to the asphalt. Peggy had snatched her from under the wheels as the bus turned. That was the day Katherine realized what it meant to be an only child: unimportant. Her friend always *said* babysitting was a pain. ("I can't go, I have to watch the brat.") But Katherine recognized her pride, her place in the business of every-day living. Peggy was wiping bloody snot off her little sister's face with her skirt, when an eighth grader told her, "You saved her life." She'd never forget the envious thrill that went through her at his words. Peggy went off in the ambulance with her sister, who was released to their parents after a checkup. When Katherine walked home alone, she felt as weightless as the dry grey skeleton leaves she waded through.

Had she gone into psychology to become solid? Katherine thought, and not for the first time, of the child inside each grownup person. If Fran's inner child was still eight, how old would hers be? Maybe sixteen — when she went to college early and discovered names for the way people felt. When she came home for Christmas, her Freshman year, she (the abstracted, bookish one), advised Peggy (the responsible, capable one) about love. Katherine had a diagnosis: "He is an introvert, and you are an extrovert. Not only that — you are a strong sensation type and he is the complete intuitive." But Peggy hadn't been too crazy about her prescription: "Either you have to learn to enjoy poetry, or find someone else who likes tennis." As for young Katherine, what did she learn to make herself solid? Names, and the ability to save her tears for when she really needed them?

She had tears in her eyes when she listened to Fran talk about her brother. Stroke-induced lability? Perhaps, but not all. Except for the first month, she has been dry, at least for her — numbed perhaps. Now what would become of a therapist who was no longer in control of her own tear ducts?

7

*W*HEN FRAN FIRST TOLD ALAN about Kathcrine's offer, he hadn't
answered her right away even though he felt delighted to have a practical problem solved — with no effort on his part. For some obscure
reason he'd wanted to mask his relief with some other real, but less
felt, concern. He'd almost said, Fran, just because you and Katherine
are friends, don't let her take advantage. Make sure you establish a
reasonable salary. Taking the free rent into consideration, it should be
. . . But he'd felt that he ought to be careful.

"You will be able to help her remain independent," he'd said, "but
she is thinking of you too. It's the perfect solution." Looking pleased
with him, she'd sealed the envelope on her notice to St. Clothilde's.

But it took a long time to elicit the details from her. Almost a month
later, Fran mentioned, a little too casually, "Katherine says there are
large picture windows." He almost laughed. That they had come to
this — on the edge of the suburbs with large picture windows. Fran
looked smug because she would have more light for her paintings.

He cleared his throat and said, "But we must remain independent,
too. This duplex — does it have separate entrances, or has it
been converted?"

"Oh, separate, I think." She smiled at him.

Fran rose with the slight wince he'd almost gotten used to — the
pregnancy, by the beginning of the second trimester, gave her an occa-
sional backache — and went into their bedroom to begin packing
boxes. It would be their third move, and he remembered how moving
exhilarated her.

Alan was so entranced with the unlikely sight and sound of Fran's
cleaning, that when his mother called he said yes, absently, to
everything she said.

"Mom wants us to come over for lunch. She has a bunch of stuff
for us."

"Alan! There's a bunch of stuff at the curb for Good Will! We don't
want any more!"

"Well, I already said we'd come over and take a look."

Alan felt dislocated, pulled backward, every time he went down the
walk toward the 1910 blue frame house that his grandmother had once
used as a rooming house. He remembered the day his family came to
live with Nona Sondini — how his mother cried! "Over selling a few
goddamned pieces of our furniture": his father's story. "It's Nona's

28

house," Leo Donnate had told his wife. If Nona, "Big Theresa," wanted them to have a *furnished* flat (with Nona's furniture, not theirs), then so be it. Once again Alan marveled at his father's simplicity: The failure of his filling station meant he didn't have a right to set policy. From then on Alan's mother returned to her childhood nickname — "Little Theresa."

Now Fran and Alan skirted the moldy rattan porch furniture (never taken in for winter), and opened the door into the narrow hall which lead to Nona's part of the house.

In the kitchen, Alan's father was already dispatching a large plate of tortellini, his head bent over his plate,his wineglass already empty. He nodded at Fran, stuck out his hand to Alan.

Alan's mother smiled. "Let me give you both a big hug!" She turned to wipe her hands on a countertop dishcloth and pieces of lettuce flew into the air. "Oh dear, oh dear. I forgot I was drying the lettuce in that towel."

Nona came to the table with four mugs of coffee. "Venite qui so sit down." She settled her own wide hips into the special chair Alan's father had remodeled for her, by padding a sturdy porch rocker. She smelled, as always, like her basil plants. Through a side door Alan could see Nona's parlor, where nothing ever changed: The curtains were always drawn, and the seashell collage of Mt. Vesuvius glowed in the dusk. He hadn't seen her bedroom, a shrine to the Infant of Prague, since he had pneumonia at ten. Her bathroom still had the odor of damp dust and Bon Ami.

"So, Alan," said his grandmother, and she gave him a long unblinking stare. Her eyes were like black currants, he thought. "I hear you're going to become a father. Maybe now you'll get a real job and stop dressing like a bum all the time in bluejeans." But her voice sounded indifferent. It was an old story — Nona's jibes. No one paid any attention. Even Fran, who had recently developed an enormous appetite for pasta, and had come to eat, it seemed. Everyone took it for granted when Nona gave him a hard time. But Alan could remember a time when Nona was his only confidant. When he came home from grade school or junior high, it was Nona, who cooked for both households, in the kitchen making mannicotti, or ravioli. "So, vieni qui, sit with me a while," she said. "Have some cake. Dolce! I bought you coke, don't tell your mother." When his mouth was full she'd ask, "Is that Jensen boy still trying to get you in trouble?" And then she listened to his day. Next he settled back for her advice. She lowered her voice. She knew. She knew about people — even children. (Other grownups knew nothing of children; it was pathetic the way his mother talked to his friends — her voice too playful.) Nona knew he had to be very careful. When a new kid entered school, he was to wait, see who spoke first. "Never show you're mad," she said, "never talk about your private business."

Alan was so immersed in the past, that he blinked when his mother said, "This is Saturday — Alan doesn't have to dress up on Saturday."

"That's right, Mom," Alan said, but he felt the old familiar stab in his colon, and hoped it wasn't too late to steer the talk away from his shortcomings as a breadwinner before his father chimed in. He searched his mind for a safe topic, but Fran said, in a dangerously sweet tone, "Alan *has* a real job. He has so many contacts with so many magazines and newspapers that last month he had to give a story to another writer." Alan tucked in an amused smile. He felt very pleased to have Fran defend him — especially as she often seemed unaware of just how he had to hustle — but they both knew why he turned down the story on new opportunities in the field of accounting. He felt a twinge of apprehension: Would he have the luxury of writing his own short stories when they had a family to feed and clothe? "Freelance writing is a business, and Alan is also a salesman," Fran said. But her condescending tone was marred by a slight burp. Alan stifled a chuckle.

Nona looked unconvinced and said, "A hen with a full nest doesn't have to cackle."

"A saying for everything, that's my favorite mother-in-law," Leo said. Alan felt relieved — the old man was in a good mood today.

Fran rolled her eyes. Alan could tell that she had used up all the wifely indignation she possessed. She seemed more amused with Nona than irritated.

"My favorite saying is, 'A little hard work with your hands never hurt anybody.' " Leo continued and looked at Alan, who glazed his eyes at his half-eaten plate of linguini Alfredo. Leo wasn't in *that* good of a mood. Yet he always managed to put up a certain front with Nona. They had this camaraderie — the practical ones in the family, but Alan wondered how his father really felt about her. How did it feel to be paying rent to her for 26 years?

Several years before he met Fran, Alan had had a falling out with Nona when he didn't follow her advice after graduating from high school. "It's sales today, boy. You shine your shoes, you buy yourself a good-looking doubleknit suit, you get a briefcase, and you have a future." Alan went to the University of Minnesota instead, and instead of majoring in business, as his Dad wanted him to do, he majored in English.

Alan noticed that his mother was fussing with her slip strap — the way she did when she got nervous. She darted a glance in his father's direction. "Larry called Leo back to work Saturdays; he said no one could get jobs done right like your father."

"Hey, that's a real compliment to you, Dad," Alan said, and thought, so now we have to sit here and listen to him talk about carburetors, and then he'll insist on taking a look at my "poor excuse for a car" — what the hell, I'll talk about what *I* want to talk about. "Larry has the lot where the Sardonnas used to live, doesn't he? The business district on Central's really extending into the old neighborhood. What ever happened to some of the families we used to know — like the Albas? Ma, didn't Mrs. Alba used to tell you some great stories?"

Little Theresa cocked her head to one side — almost the way she used to do, Alan thought — and said, "Yes, I seem to remember . . ." Alan felt pleased to have distracted his mother from her perennial task of pleasing everyone and averting all unpleasantness. She used to have more mischief, and used to gather funny bits of gossip around the neighborhood. In his sophomore year, she'd broken her leg on a loose tread and, when it didn't heal right, stopped going out so much. Now she looked more wispy every year and she didn't have many new stories.

"Yes," she said, "I remember Cora Alba's great grandmother saw a ghost, a cowboy who walked through the screen on her kitchen door while she was ironing late one August night in 1905."

Leo pulled his shirt out over his belt, leaned back in his chair and winked at Nona.

"That Alba woman used to put something in her coffee besides sugar," Nona said, and she nudged her son-in-law.

Nothing had changed. His mother looked flustered, and she pushed back the frizz of her graying bangs. But then she, with great daring, winked at Alan.

Until he was seventeen, Alan had laughed at his mother too. He couldn't remember, exactly, why he went over to the other side. Perhaps because he'd inherited her story telling. Nona, on the other hand, wanted everything "up-to-date." The phrase, "expense account," used as an adjective, was her highest compliment. "Your shirt — it's real expense account." What that meant exactly, Alan didn't know. Maybe Nona thought that salesmen didn't have to take two jobs to go to college. With only eight to ten hours a semester, it had taken him almost seven years to get his degree. By that time he had added a J-school minor. And he came home with ethnic human interest on his mind — feature stories, short stories, but Nona wouldn't talk to him.

31

Living at home became impossible. Nona was implacable when you didn't take her advice. She let him wait for the dire consequences in silence. "I say things once; if you don't want to listen, too bad."

He was banished from the wood-burning stove, hot coffee, suppa, opal basil, licorice smell of fennel, tea kettle cosy, conspiracy. His mother was not a good conspirator. She seemed not to realize they were allies.

Now Alan shook himself out of his reverie and put his arm around his mother's boney shoulders. "Mom, how about if I come over some day and we'll talk about the old neighborhood? There's a story I'd like to do."

"Good, Alan, I'd like that, but now . . ." She glanced over at Alan's father, who was telling Nona a Norwegian joke. She rose suddenly to her feet. "We better get something over with. Leo, please come up and help Alan and me with those things I have for them. No, Frances you stay right there, you shouldn't strain yourself." Little Theresa sounded almost severe, but her voice finished on a huff — as if she'd run out of air. She had two high round spots of color on her cheeks, and she didn't look at Nona.

Alan heard his mother's keys click together as they climbed the narrow stairs to the Donnate's upstairs flat. Alan's mother said she kept the door to their part of the house locked because the downstairs entrance opened onto Jackson Street and all the unemployed hoods. But Alan didn't believe that was the real reason. When Nona left the kitchen, hoisting her corseted bulk with an angry moan at each step, she knocked with a rat-a-tat-tat. She came to coddle, to admonish. She knocked often.

The upholstery of the rose loveseat was in perfect condition, but clouds of dust rose as the two men set it down with a thud on the landing, so they could rest. As a child, Alan's favorite spot was the landing. He wondered why — perhaps because it was in between his parents' place and Nona's. No one else claimed it, so it was his — neutral ground. For some reason, it was winter he remembered from his childhood. As soon as he knocked the snow off his boots onto the rug, he always went straight to the landing, pulled a Twinkie out of his school bag and took his book off the window sill where he'd left it that morning. Then he sat in the one spot of sunlight, his back against the wall, the radiator hissing and steaming. What was he reading? *Twenty Thousand Leagues Under the Sea*, maybe, or *The Hardy Boys Break Camp*.

When they went through the kitchen, Alan peeked above the overstuffed cushions with what he hoped was a disarmingly comic diffidence. He couldn't decide who was more surprised — Nona or Fran.

"Alan!" she cried, and then bit her lower lip. Little Theresa was coming down the stairs with two lamps and an end table. And she beamed with defiance and generosity.

"I've borrowed Uncle Louie's trailer," his mother said.

Alan looked at Fran. With his eyebrows, he signaled "We'll talk later."

After five trips up and down the stairs, he said, "Thanks, Mom, but is there enough left for you and Dad?"

"Oh, there always was too much, and it's mostly Nona's extras, anyway. I like it better this way, with the paths gone." When he wrinkled his forehead, she smiled and said, "You know — between the first layer of furniture and the second."

When they unloaded the last of Little Theresa's bounty, Alan looked around their apartment, now temporarily furnished with one of Nona's bottom layers. A hybrid. He called to Fran, "It will be nice to live in a new place!"

She came back into the room, trailing the dusty drapes she'd ripped right off the windows. She was laughing, weakly. They'd both run out of disposal ideas. And who would want to hurt Little Theresa's feelings? "I thought you liked older places — with atmosphere!" Fran was choking with laughter.

Like was not the word. They had inherited atmosphere — like a piling collecting barnacles. Now if only they could transplant Nona's closets and crawlspaces to Katherine's new house. If only they could hide the furniture of his past, make it disappear. The old house could absorb anything. Nona's place was full of stops and starts: filled-in doors, walls torn down one year and put back in the next. Alan often tried to remember the floor plan from the time of his childhood, and he seemed to remember that an inner staircase was unused, except for her canning jars and old issues of the *Farmer's Almanac* and *Readers' Digest.*

The truth was — he and Fran had been living for 11 years like perpetual undergraduates. That was why they were open to such outrageous intrusions on the part of his family. Well, people could change; he and Fran could learn to be less . . . exposed? Alan thought of their friends, Sally and Ellis, who'd lived together from Introductory English Literature until Sally's post grad year at Oxford. Eight years. Then they got married. Not long after that, they'd discarded the red, black, and yellow Indian challis throw covering the day bed. Next they threw out the day bed and bought a bedroom set. Finally, they framed their art deco prints. Once Alan would have bet on twenty years for their own prints, frayed at the edges and moved to a house in the country maybe. But the kitchen floor there would have the same

33

1,000 layers of all-in-one clean and polish, each layer laminating in the dirt. A fine patina of age.

He reflected that Fran's approach to the detritus of every day living took strict discipline — for a person so inclined to order. He smiled to himself at the thought of the bread-board covering their sink of dirty dishes, the bed spread pulled up over a jumble of shoes, shirts, and blankets. Just like her mail: Everything went into a large manila envelope. If, after three months, she didn't remember what was inside, she figured it could all be thrown away.

Were there two kinds of people in this world — those who changed their lives and those who shrugged a little, stretched a little, patched a hole or two, making their lives fit like an outgrown suit of clothes? It wasn't hard for him to see where he and Fran were heading before the baby. And even now, he wasn't sure if they'd found a new pattern. He couldn't be as openly enthusiastic as he sometimes felt about becoming a father. Once he told her that having children would fulfill him. How irritated she was — as if he'd accused her. Being Fran, she hadn't admitted she disliked fulfilling other people's expectations: making his parents grandparents, and so forth. And she hadn't admitted that she worried about taking the next developmental step. All Fran would say, stubbornly, was, "Alan, that's just not it."

He could hear her singing as she tossed old shoes out of the closet, into a box for Good Will. Perhaps it would work out. Maybe she wouldn't mind having furniture after all.

Enough of Fran. He got out a manuscript he was to critique for a local press. It was his second, this time rather cursory, reading. On the first page he wrote, "We like your story, but the character of George tends to be somewhat flat or symmetrical. Perhaps you could develop him in this way:" He stopped. Was that too directive? Well, what were editors for? But he couldn't concentrate.

So he opened his file cabinet and took out a folder with a short story manuscript of his own: A major character, Peter, was to function as a foil for the other two characters. The two dominant traits of Peter's personality were a need to control and an awe of mystery. Naturally, these two traits would work at cross-purposes to each other. A provocative approach, he thought, and felt sure that it had worked well for him in the past, although it was not altogether original. He seemed to remember borrowing the idea from Elizabeth Hanford Johnson. Anyway — did his Peter wear a hat? Speak with a Midwest accent?

Alan flicked the throw rug to one side, put his palms flat on the floor, kicked his legs up into a hand stand.

Fran emerged from the hall walk-in closet. "Alan, stop fooling around and come in here to help me."

"I'm working."

"I see that. So am I."

Out with the broken kites, bent armatures. First the periphery, frippery. Keep the rocker. "A good sign," said Alan.

Muttering over hats, yanking bell-bottomed pants from their hangers at last. "This is enough to give decision-making a bad name," Fran told him. Easier to jettison almost everything.

"But not the crock pot, Fran!"

"Cutting up all those vegetables takes too much time," she

Alan had never seen much resemblance between his mother and his wife until Fran decided to shed some layers. She organized a garage sale before they left their old apartment. He pretended to faint away on the kitchen floor when she finally noticed their dusty wine-making paraphernalia above the cupboard. "Alan, we'll never be homesteaders. This has got to go."

In their half of the duplex, all the walls had to be white. Fran sighed over curved wooden dowels. "A Zen environment?" Alan asked. A vase on the table in the "spare room" was to have one milkweed pod, five straw flowers. Alan looked around and said, "Maybe we should go to a few garage sales. Get some clothes and stuff for the baby." Fran glared.

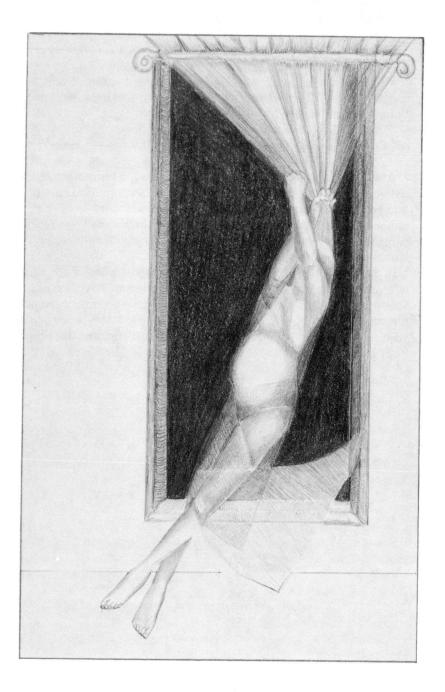

8

A CURVING WEIGHT, a lower center of gravity. If someone were to try to push her over, she'd pop forward — like one of those inflated Bozo dolls: Fran didn't think about her pregnancy, but, by the fourth month, she felt it always.

In early September, she and Alan opened the curiously light (hollow-centered) door to their duplex. Unreal. Like an architect's cardboard model. Fran set her box down and sat upon it. The empty room should have seemed large. She thought, if I keep increasing this way, I'll stay in the center of the room and the walls will come to me. Like Alice in Wonderland. Just that unpleasant. She opened the window.

A hot dry wind — more like spring than late summer. "I don't like the weather today," Fran said. "It makes me feel restless."

Alan came up behind her, put his arm around her waist. "But it's kind of nice to be making a new beginning." She heard his unspoken cliche — "a new beginning in a place of our own." Katherine would be moving in two weeks, after they got her side and theirs ready. It wasn't a place of their own,and she wondered if he'd come to mind that.

Fran's nasal passages felt sore. "This wind — here we are in the Midwest and it makes me think of the chinook off the mountains in northern Montana. It's like the foehn that Katherine's sister hates because it gives her headaches." She leaned on the window ledge and felt grit on her hands. The wind — whipping sand through the mesh in the screen — moaned into an ever-rising whine rounding the house: Now, now, now, who, when, wheeeeeeeee. Now what? Unpack and wait.

Toward evening, when they had opened half their boxes, the lights began to come on across the road and they felt exposed by the curtainless windows. Fran held a sheet to the window while Alan fastened it to the frame with a staple gun. Perspiration trickled down their temples. The wind had stopped, "as if stoppered," Alan said, "as if sucked with a whoosh down some large genie bottle." The night would be a bell jar.

At three A.M., Fran came up out of sleep dripping wet, and pulling frantically at her nightgown. The aura of the nightmare — so evil, so fateful, was still there: She and Alan had been in a large empty room, cutting long strips of cloth to hang either side of the floor-to-ceiling window. They worked obsessively because the time of some frightening event was edging closer: someone, something, would force the window open. All at once — the wind! Not from outside, but from within the room. And the cloth of the curtain clung to Fran's hands as if beginning to grow there. curling up and around her, like a skin she couldn't tear away.

9

"LET'S GET THIS DOUBLE HOUSEHOLD organized," said Alan, so they decided that they would eat together every Wednesday and Sunday in Fran and Alan's apartment. Katherine appreciated Alan's sensitivity. She was the one who presented problems, so she could hardly suggest any sort of communal life . . . And it made her feel good that they wanted to be with her socially. After all, she was also their common *work* . . . The mix of relationships and roles hardly bore thinking of . . .

On Sunday evening of their first week together, Katherine knew that a second glass of wine had pasted a fond, silly smile upon her face. She thought, I'm relieved to discover I like Alan. Then she caught herself: I wasn't at all worried that he'd like me! Because I've always been able to control any emotional situation with my ability to name it? It's arrogant, but the old confidence is still there — stroke or no stroke.

It was obvious from Fran's unusual vivacity ("Alan, tell Katherine about the time we hitchhiked through Yugoslavia and Albania.") that she too, had feared there might be conflict. But Alan has always liked to read psychology. For the past year, he has been excited about what he calls, "the straight-forward approach" of Behaviorism. "But that's so contradictory, Alan," Fran protested. "Behaviorists don't want to talk about underlying causes, and you love to go on about childhood influences. Sometimes I think you own my childhood because of your superior interest in it."

When Alan asked about Katherine's psychological philosophy she said, "Eclectic! But I think I get the most from Jung. He doesn't tell me to merely relieve the symptoms, which do have a purpose. We hurt for a reason." She massaged the fingers of her left hand, and looked at Fran. "But depth psychology can do much harm, if the psychologist is not humble, and tries to probe someone's mind and emotions like a scientist."

"Then, how does the therapist cure the patient?" Alan asked.

"The therapist doesn't cure the patient. The healing power is there within the self, the soul. Dreams come to guide us, and they need to become a part of our daily consciousness: The day needs the night. But the danger in depth psychology comes from the fact that, as Jung says, 'The psyche is weightlessness itself.'"

Alan got up for a cigarette, the way he always did, Katherine observed, when he was feeling tense. She wondered if she had been guilty of jargon. But Alan was only intensely interested. Katherine was touched to realize he believed there was truth in what she said, if only he could come to understand it.

Whenever Alan wanted to discuss *Symbols of Transformation*, Fran smiled and said, "Mystical," but she listened.

Once, while Alan and Katherine were talking about the necessity of becoming more conscious, Fran got up, and went to her studio for a painting, which she propped against the refrigerator where they could study it:

A glowing white disc with a silvered-green cast gradually shading into a neutral containing red and green, a no-color color, which continued to darken as it rounded, and disappeared into red. The globe floated on a field of pale orange at the top of the picture plane, darkening in imperceptible progression into deep blue.

They looked at the picture in silence, which, Katherine saw, Fran took as the highest compliment.

10

BY FRAN'S EIGHTH MONTH, their double household was established in a routine. It was often Alan now who drove Katherine to therapy and assisted her when necessary in her office. She had, with reluctance, referred three-fourths of her patients to four colleagues in the hopes that her lightened caseload would enable her to get on with a major task: becoming independent.

Only another disabled person, Katherine thought, could understand how much effort must go into the minute details of every day living. Then she shook her head at herself. Alan and Fran have done everything they possibly could do. But it was like wading upstream in a long skirt, or one of those dreams in which time is so sticky, so slow, you can see the minutes pull apart: A slow-motion photo of a sprinter, muscles stretched, contracted, face in a grimace. That's me, Katherine decided, and I've only gone from the wheelchair to the toilet.

Her bathroom was arranged so that after Fran helped her out of the tub, she could finish by herself: Her toothbrush, comb, and deodorant were all where she could reach them. A bar next to the toilet, and another in the shower. In the kitchen she could reach the coffee, milk, bread and tea, et cetera, on the lower shelves. Fran found a hot plate and instant coffee warmer, and Alan installed a long hose in the sink for washing up.

Planning for the life of the body! Only one other time was so given over to maintenance — when Emma was a baby. Katherine had never wanted to learn the contents of another person's bowels. But soon she was following Emma's elimination with interest. She had to. With infant diarrhea came the danger of dehydration. So it was clear liquids on a schedule. But Emma developed a high fever. A sunken look around her eyes. Projectile vomiting. A frantic visit to the doctor. Perhaps the breast milk was too rich. Sugar water, a week of dilute formula. Despite the breast pump, Katherine developed milk fever — her breasts sore, hot and hard. Almost had to stop nursing that time. and while she was trying to keep her milk and provide other liquids — an endless number of bottles to sterilize. She wondered if her recent memory was suffering: Such total recall from the past was symptomatic of brain damage. She hadn't thought about the constraints of baby care in years.

Yet, little by little, she was making some physical progress. Her emotional state was another story. Since leaving St. Clothilde she has been shocked by her own mood swings. Just yesterday she snapped at Fran because she put the tape recorder on the left side of the desk before a session. Frequently, after Fran left to work in her studio, Katherine was repentant. Thrown by frustration into self-consciousness, she cataloged her own symptoms: "Decreased inhibition is a common result of a right brain insult." It didn't help much. But it did help to think of herself as she was described in therapy: I'm like the kid who gets around holding onto furniture. Reach out, lunge, almost fall, catch myself. Walking is an amazing feat — a balancing act with which I intend to amaze my adult self.

11

DURING THE DAY Fran's work went well. But nights it seemed as if a part of herself were splitting off. In her dreams, the baby was already born and she kept leaving him behind, only to find him later, but damaged: swollen eyes, nose pushed to one side, spattered with mud. Once she forgot she'd put their child into her suitcase. When she remembered, she opened it and found the baby pinched together, his head twisted — crushed by a pair of shoes belonging to Fran's mother.

Most of her dreams were a part of some long journey — interrupted by day — toward an unknown destination. She traveled by water or, more usually, by car at an insane speed. Safety, a condition of fate, always came just in time — at the edge of a cliff, or the bank of a flooding river.

The only previous journey dream she remembered had come on the day of her brother's funeral. Early that morning Fran overheard her grandma tell her mother, "She's eight, way too young for a funeral." Her mother was crying, so it was hard to hear what she said except for the words, "closed casket." Fran wasn't too young to understand. Michael was hurt so bad that no one could stand to see his face. Ever again.

While the grownups were at the funeral, three year old Mark sat on the babysitter's lap, and Fran fell into an exhausted sleep. She dreamed that no one was left but her mother when the black spaceship came, and her mother said, "Don't be afraid, your life has been good," so she was not sad but happy and the trip was — a rushing on the wind.

12

EVERY OTHER SATURDAY Katherine's friend, Mitzi Neufrauw, also a clinical psychologist, took her to a good restaurant. Katherine's old favorite was La Maison Bleu (a small menu, French country cuisine). When Mitzi wheeled her through the door, on her first outing since she left St. Clothilde's, Katherine felt self-conscious. She tried to focus on Mitzi's appreciation of the intimate atmosphere, only eighteen tables, each set with fresh daisies. So familiar, yet so unreal. Precious. A protected world, where any wood is hand rubbed, where secondhand furniture gets antique respect. The patrons of La Maison Bleu, in their consignment shop cardigans, costume shop-jersey knits, wide of shoulder and discreetly smelling of moth balls, loved estate sales. They played at being poor, and did it beautifully. Katherine thought of her friends at St. Clothilde's : Mrs. Nelson's handstitched quilts, Miss Bundy's armoire, Ms. Dickson's family home — all gone to the thrift shops. In room 306-C, Ms. Dickson saved two small oils from her "liquidation," as she put it. But, as the residence forbade nails in the walls, she had to prop them against the mirror, upon the metal dresser.

Katherine tried not to think of the last time she was in La Maison Bleu, the evening of her stroke, when she embarrassed herself with loud complaints about the pilaf. Coming here again had been a deliberate decision to face a little unpleasantness. The longer she waited, the more difficult it would be. After all, she had been coming here three times a week for ten years.

"Your face is flushed, Katherine," Mitzi said. "Do you feel a little warm?" Ah, friends. She could tell her almost anything important, but she was too vain to tell her about her human foolishness. "I'm fine, Mitzi." How to say that she'd been overcome with gratitude: Ellen, the waitress that night, who had taken her plate back to the kitchen two times, dear Ellen had given her a hug and a kiss after settling them at her usual table.

The other half of the restaurant was given over to oak tables where the regulars played board games. Katherine remembered how she used to like coming alone because she felt free to take a newspaper off the rack and read. Sometimes she brought a book from home. Other times she played chess or just talked with the others. She had liked the feeling that, if she chose, the acquaintances she made could be her friends. But somehow, it had been more agreeable to have that as a possibility.

44

Why had she never brought Mitzi before? Perhaps she'd never be able to come here alone again. And was that so bad?

"Alan and Fran are so transparent," Katherine said, while they were waiting for their menus. "They are so glad to see me get out." She didn't tell Mitzi her real concern, that she could imagine Alan saying, "You know, Fran, if she didn't have other friends, it would be quite a responsibility for us." Katherine shrugged that thought away. *She* felt responsible for *them.* "But I'm so concerned about this pregnancy, Fran's ambivalence! It's like I'm going to become a grandmother."

While waiting for their salads, Mitzi asked, "Is Fran's mother going to help out when the baby comes?"

"No, she has a policy of only coming for the second grandchildren. Fran says her mother figures that there wouldn't be enough for her to do without a toddler to watch. But I think Fran needs her, and doesn't know how to tell her that. She said, 'My mother is always talking about how easy it is to give birth, how she had all her babies after two labor pains.'

"Fran's feelings about her mother are in a state of flux just now," Katherine added. "Maybe it's all for the best. Alan will be there and his mother will help. I'll be there for her . . ." Katherine finished her coffee, regretting the caffeine. "Mitzi, I'm worried — these nightmares she's been having. I have her permission to discuss this with you. I need your advice." Advice! She needed Mitzi to go *anywhere*, and she wanted to go straight home and talk to Fran about those dreams. But Fran was her employee, and she shouldn't also be her patient. No — that was a foolish evasion. She was glad that Fran's mother wasn't coming to be with her, so she, Katherine, could be her mother. She was not objective. She ordered wine.

"Katie, you have never been a purist about analytical objectivity. So, you start with a double projection. But you know it. You might help her. Who else could help her?"

Katherine took another bite of her ragout before replying. "You?"

Mitzi shook her head. "I have too many of your old patients to take on any new ones."

Katherine wasn't surprised. It seemed Fran was her task.

"Where does Alan fit in?" Mitzi asked.

"Despite Alan's new interest in the unconscious, he's too reasonable. He thinks if only I'd show Fran why she is afraid, that then she can decide to be sensible. But she already knows why she's disturbed. Knowing makes no difference. I think she has to go through a transformation."

Such a dramatic statement, and in such a place. Across the room

45

someone said, "Check." The click, click of stones at the backgammon table. Rosy shades directing the light downward to illuminate only what was held in the hand.

Katherine leaned forward. "The question is — should I be there too? You see I'm running a risk. It's dangerous to interfere. Do you know the book, *Boundaries of the Soul* by the Jungian psychologist, June Singer? Her training analyst warned Singer of over-involvement, and said that a psychotherapist was not supposed to want the patient to get well."

"Whatever does that mean?"

"It means, I think, that I must never do for Fran what she should do for herself. Only Fran knows when she is ready to give up her symptoms — being blown away, losing her baby in the wind. Perhaps she should, in some sense, enter the wind."

"No one should do that alone. It seems you're the person to help her because you're so determined not to write the script."

"Oh, yes, but that was the analyst speaking. As someone who would like to be her mother, I just want her to be happy. I'd like to say, 'Fran, all of us are crazy being women. It's normal. It doesn't help to be a mother. That's double crazy. But we get through it.'"

"Well, tell her that too."

Katherine looked down at her lap and laughed at what she saw. Her big freckled hands had folded her napkin into a diaper.

13

WHEN FRAN FIRST FELT the baby move, she didn't tell him. He felt cheated, but she said, "It was so delicate, like a flutter, I thought I was imagining it."

Fran grew larger, and the baby shifted in gross movements, distorting one side and then the other of her "gravid oval belly" — a nice phrase, Alan thought as he wrote it down. He put his mouth to the swelling and said, "Your father says, quiet down in there!"

"A typical Donnate male! You're getting strict already," she teased him.

"Never!" He dropped back onto the rug at her feet, his arms flat on either side of him. He grunted — as if he were winded. How much did Fran listen to him, really? He would never be like his father.

"Alan. One minute you're making jokes, and the next minute you're offended."

It was true. Fran had complained about losing her second trimester hormonal serenity. In the last month, the baby was like a heavy parcel she wanted to put down. So did Alan. He gained weight and was always tired. And he also became tired of Fran's self-absorption. Why didn't she ever ask about his past, about his family? He was tired of his part in their marital dialogue — the interpreting, the commentary.

But Fran was the one who had picked up on his hyper-participation in her pregnancy. She informed him that his involvement was a condition know as couvade. "Alan, you've had every symptom I've had. When I was queasy, you said you were getting the flu. When my ankles were swollen, you said you must have twisted yours running." Actually, Katherine had mentioned the phenomenon to Fran, who obviously enjoyed being able to educate Alan for a change. "It's expected in primitive tribes," she said, "for the father to go into labor with the mother, and it doesn't mean holding her hand. He has the labor pains too."

Alan thought that was going too far. He felt angry and a little self-conscious because Fran discussed him with Katherine — like Dagwood Bumstead, the bumbling, hypochondriac male. Fran had as much sensitivity as the calico cat they'd banished to Katherine's side to avoid the risk of toxoplasmosis during the pregnancy. This place or that — it was all the same to the cat. His psyche or hers — was all the same to Fran.

His father would have hooted, if he'd known that Alan picked the obstetrician when Fran said she would barely be able to tolerate the checkups and didn't want to talk about the birth. Alan chose Dr. Marcus because she practiced the Le Boyer method of delivery. "Boy what?" asked Fran.

"It's named after this French obstetrician who realized how babies must suffer when they are born in the traditional way. Think how awful birth is for the baby! All of a sudden — out of the warm dark into the cold light of a large white room — like an astronaut set adrift in space. Except that nobody turns the astronaut upside down and slaps him. The light blinds the baby. And the noise! The baby is used to the muffled slow, slow as blood, voices of his mother or father. Then all of a sudden — the barking of efficient grownups doing their job in a way that is most comfortable to them — never mind the child. What a welcome!"

"So what does Le Boyer do to make it better for the baby?"

"Everyone speaks in whispers and they dim the lights, and turn down the air conditioning. As soon as the baby is born, the doctor will place him on your breast, and he can nurse." Fran looked doubtful, but Alan pretended not to notice. "No — I got the order wrong — as soon as the baby is born, she gives the baby to me, and I hold him in a warm bath, and *then* I give him to you."

"Him? In a warm bath?"

"Well, him or her — gave myself away, didn't I! The warm bath is because the baby finds the cold room painful, and it's a good transition from the womb, where she'd been swimming around for nine months."

And that was almost the way it was. When Dr. Marcus gave her to him, he almost dropped her, she was so slippery, and he'd just been mortally disconcerted: The doctor handed him a surgical scissors, and he realized she expected him to cut the chord. The connection with Fran was severed in an instant, a slicing, his hand shook, the cord pulsed, and Caitlin yowled. As soon as he slide her into the warm water, one hand under her small bottom, one hand under her head and shoulders, she stopped crying. And looked up at him, looked straight into his eyes and greeted him.

PART TWO

14

Alan brought his mother along the day he came to take Fran and the baby home. She almost trotted down the corridor of the hospital, her head forward, and he could see how much it meant — his asking her to come.

Fran was waiting in the armchair beside the bed, already dressed in her bluejeans, which now closed, and the voluminous sweatshirt she had worn to avoid purchasing maternity clothes. "I told them to let the baby sleep as long as she could . . ."

Just then a nurse came in with Caitlin, who was crying and waving her fists. Fran dropped the magazine she was holding and held out her arms, but stiffly, her elbows to her waist. She drew the baby toward her slowly, as if her arms retracted. "I can't remember what side she had last," Fran said, and pulled up her sweatshirt. Alan was amused when his mother rose and walked over to the window.

"How high it is up here! It's nothing like the place where you were born, Alan — a dark back bedroom at the midwife's."

Fran looked over at the window. "This is *too* high — like giving birth in a skyscraper."

Mother can sit down now that Fran has settled into nursing Cait, Alan thought. On the way over to the hospital she told him, "I'm not going to be one of these interfering mother-in-laws. I'm not going to start giving Frances advice every time she looks the least bit uncertain."

"Oh, I almost forgot," his mother said, after an awkward ten minutes, "I brought you a present." She bent and rummaged through the large carryall at her feet.

She looked at Fran. "Shall I open it for you, or could I hold the baby now while you do it?"

"Here. Burp her for me."

His mother had to lean way over to take the baby. Fran unwrapped the box and drew out a corduroy navy blue pouch or purse with dangling straps and strings. She looked puzzled, wrinkling her forehead as she smiled.

"It's a Snugli," his mother explained. "You use it to carry the baby close to your heart. The idea is that it's like the womb, and makes the baby feel secure. We didn't have anything like that in my day."

Fran burst into tears. "Oh, thank you so much. You can't know how worried I've been about taking the baby home. The freeway, those semis barreling along, our little Volkswagon, and it seemed I should hold her, but I knew it would be safer if she were in a baby seat — and those all seem to be for bigger children."

"Why, Fran," said Alan, "I didn't realize you . . ." He grabbed some kleenex, dabbed at her face.

"You've got the baby blues," his mother said, handing the baby back to Frances. "Use the other side now, dear, or you'll be sore. These days they say it's hormones, but it happened to me three days after I had Alan when the happiness wore off and it first hit me — You, Theresa Donnate, are responsible for this tiny little person, who might break if you . . . But listen to me rattling on about myself. You'll be all right, Frances, every woman goes through this."

"Thank you. Really. Now I can put the seatbelt on my lap for the two of us and there's no way she could fly out of my arms."

On the trip home, Alan traveled ten miles per hour slower than usual, and he kept glancing back at Fran's face in the rear view mirror. His mother had said, "Oh Frances, you must sit in the front seat next to Alan; I always hated it when my mother assumed, as the older woman, that she should sit next to my husband in front — with me in back like a poor relation!" But Fran wanted to be in back where it was "statistically safer."

Alan was amazed at his mother. He hadn't ever heard her talk so much, without prompting, about her own feelings. And now she was bestowing the wealth of birth and motherhood stories she'd collected upon Fran, who sat behind them, her chin tucked over the baby's head, looking out the window at speeding cars and trucks, lanechangers, four ton semis, regarding them all with aplomb. Did Fran feel the baby was now safe because it was, once again, attached to her?

Fran listened to his mother's stories — Maria Bono and her tap-dancing triplets, Nancy Kelly and the spastic son she raised to become a national merit scholar winner — and he imagined that she might find them comforting. But then she didn't seem to pay particular attention until his mother told about the girl next door who had a nervous breakdown after her second child. "She ran over to get me one day, carrying the baby, the two year old pulled along by one arm, and all three of them crying. She was afraid of sticking the baby with a pin, afraid of scalding him in the bath water, afraid she'd somehow hurt him. She had to go away for a while to a state hospital, and then when she came back she saw a psychiatrist, but she got better, she did get better. She didn't have any more children though."

Alan watched Fran in the mirror. She slowly rubbed her chin over the downy top of the baby's head, folded her arms across the round mound under her cape, and closed her eyes.

15

KATHERINE NOTICED THAT FRAN moved as if under water. She put the baby in her Snugli and the baby slept while she did housework. Doing the dishes, she would pause, then walk over to the window to look out at the still-frozen river. She didn't go near her brushes all of March.

When the ice broke, Fran went to her easel, "wearing" the baby in the Snugli. She found it tiring to reach across even such a small weight, so she didn't work long. Alan commented to Katherine that his wife seemed indecisive, reworking passages until her colors turned to mud.

"She worked better when she was pregnant," Alan said.

"I asked her why she didn't put the baby down," Katherine said, "and she told me she liked carrying her."

Alan shook his head. "She's still pregnant."

It was an early, hot summer when the baby was only four months old, so he purchased an air conditioner. But Fran insisted that the baby would be chilled. She sat with her in the blue room Alan had prepared, hour upon hour, one nursing session flowing into another. Mother and baby woke and dozed. Fran read the children's books she'd collected, taking her time over *The Secret Garden*. She refused to look at the newspaper.

"I think they're in some sort of cocoon," Alan remarked to Katherine.

She looked at him with concern. "Do you get enough time with the baby?"

"Oh, yes, Fran doesn't exclude me; on the contrary, she's more expressive, wants to talk more. That is, when she's not sleepwalking, when I'm not sleepwalking."

The baby woke frequently at night. Katherine told Mitzi she always heard the clumsy movements of the parents. "If I told them, 'Let Caitlin make a few sounds! Don't worry about how that baby sleeps at night, or if she cries a little!' they wouldn't listen anyway." She couldn't tell Mitzi what really made her diffident: To Fran she was a "childless" woman how could she give practical advice about babies? "I'm afraid Fran will have an anxiety attack from lack of sleep. They can't go on monitoring the child's breathing . . ." Even to herself, Katherine sounded agitated. Mitzi, who had known her for almost thirty-five years, looked concerned. About my professional objectivity? wondered Katherine. If so, she had good reason . . . To forstall Mitzi's obvious but, so far, unspoken question — Did Fran know about Emma? — Katherine babbled on: "I do agree that you can't, in any emotional sense, spoil a baby, and yet — they circle around her; they are her satellites."

"Well, you know how to be tactful," Mitzi said, and she narrowed her eyes. Thank *you* for your tact, thought Katherine.

Katherine watched Fran for signs of fatigue. Actually it was Alan who became irritable. He was not able to go back to sleep after Caitlin woke them. He nodded, without the relaxation of drowsiness, over his copy in the daytime. "It's like I put a tranquilizer in my coffee," he complained. As a defense, Katherine thought, he'd begun joking about couvade before Caitlin's birth. She suspected it had continued beyond labor with him. Perhaps, lagging a little behind Fran — for all her problems — he might still be in the early stages of postpartum, and sometimes a little depressed. But he told Katherine, when he was feeling low, that all he had to do was hold Caitlin, and everything was — timeless. She just was. In touching her, her silken skin, he took a deep breath and his worries just flowed out as he exhaled.

Fran handled the sleep deprivation by daydreaming; often her eyes seemed unfocused. For all her fears, she had some useful coping mechanisms, Katherine thought. If only she herself could have had some rest with her own baby! Sometimes it wasn't so unhealthy to retreat. Max had said to her, after Emma developed colic," "Katie, just accept the crying. Don't fight for normal time. This will pass. It's like being in combat."

But Katherine hadn't been able to stifle a feeling of, well — rage. She felt harassed — not by Emma, but the situation, and her anger, she guessed now, had been turned back in upon herself.

When Emma wasn't screaming, Katherine liked to look into her eyes: She looked right back. A serious small person. And when the baby suffered, Katherine felt an ache of pity. Babies were locked into their bodies. Their fear was inchoate. But Katherine's anger did have a focus: She no longer had the time or energy to work.

During her pregnancy she had decided to revise her dissertation and submit it to some New York publishers rather than to the more scholarly university presses. She thought she might have a gift for clarification. But that was only after she emerged from what she thought of as her cotton box in those first three months of pregnancy: their king-sized bed with the yellow chenille spread, she sinking down into pillows every day in early afternoon with a pack of index cards and a stack of books, and waking, drugged, one hour later, when she'd force herself to take notes. But in the last six months before Emma was born, she felt herself growing firm and clear, even as the baby grew.

The shape she made while sitting, thighs apart, supporting the baby: a spring bulb — layered from the inside out, the shape she made was rooted. And her thesis, like a flowering stalk, sent out one blossom after another. She knew she was a writer. "The great time dissolver," she said to Max one day when he came home at six, and she realized that she hadn't moved from her chair.

Then Emma, her insistant mouth pulling at the breast. The squeaking sibilance of milk going in . . . But the doctor had explained, "That's the sound of immature breathing. Her trachea hasn't fully closed. It's not unusual, and happens even to large babies like Emma. She'll catch up in a month or so. It's nothing to worry about." Katherine remembered all his reassurances, from all those years ago.

Emma had one cold after another. Katherine never heard normal infant respiration. The night Emma stopped breathing, Katherine woke at 3 A.M. The silence.

She didn't remember how long it took her to cry. She did remember being wrenched, nauseated. It was (a black thought), like the worst of morning sickness. Her mother, Max, the doctor, all insisted she must cry. ("It will do you good.") But there wasn't any room inside her chest. Every breath burned — like sub-zero cold. The doctor gave her pills to dry the milk. Her breasts, sore and hard, finally softened. But her breath was still shallow — there wasn't any room. To feel. When she took a pill, her thoughts played on — the surface of her mind like Muzak by Valium. She'd rather have the pain.

Emma was not to be. Katherine's life would resume the only course she had ever been able to imagine for herself: scholarship, writing, and — the most creative part — working with patients.

"Thirty is still young." How many times did people tell her that. Implication: time for other children. But she'd been given a sign: Emma died. If only the baby would become, in time, some quiescent dream, some different woman's dream. But Emma did not bear thinking of; Katherine had born her once.

After their first grief, Katherine and Max did not speak of Emma's death. They hadn't planned her birth: at twenty, and even thirty, fertility meant publication. At first her pregnancy had stunned her, seemed unreal. When she recovered, her reaction was: Of course — a baby. Within a month, she had become used to the idea, and so, was offended when Mitzi, who thought Katherine was depressed, asked if she had considered an abortion. Not a religious stand, just instinct. Restful — to surrender oneself to a process.

In the last trimester of her pregnancy, Katherine had a patient she still remembered with affection and pride. She knew she could not have helped the young woman, who was terrified of her three-months pregnancy, if she had not accepted her own condition. The patient had been abused by her mother as a child, and feared that she too would be abusive. Katherine told her that she was already a good mother. Didn't she eat the most nutritious foods? Didn't she get enough rest, take vitamins, give up smoking and alcohol? Did she know she could massage the baby in the womb? Did she know babies could hear their mother's voice? (Katherine was, at the time, stretching things a bit; but she was gratified twenty years later to read of evidence that babies did, indeed, respond to their mothers in the womb.) "Your conscious mind is telling you, 'Be careful, be afraid,'" Katherine said, "while your unconscious mind is saying, in your dreams, 'relax — I welcome new life.' " It was Katherine's first personal experience with dreams of pregnancy: Bridges over baths, and every ocean was . . . contained outside an island by an island.

It was a pleasure from the first for Katherine to enter the experience of her patients: Quiet listening without possessiveness — her talent. She had a joyful respect for her own serenity, and was glad she could, so easily, leave her own problems behind. She could become someone else, but she didn't hurt with her patients. Instead, she liked to think she encouraged the spiritual core of each sufferer, the part of the psyche that watched, and learned.

After Emma's death, Katherine's entry into the lives of her patients seemed more and more like an escape. All her life she'd disliked passing over her own uneasy feelings: *Now something bothers me. What is it? Oh, yes, it was her frown* . . . and then she'd move on, happy she'd picked up another psychic stitch.

After Emma's death, she found that her habitual state was emotional opacity. Like a mirror re-silvered to hide a major flaw. She was a psychologist who would not name her feelings. So, gradually, after a year or so of counseling, she allowed Emma to remain, just on the edge of consciousness. Now, before each session she whispered "Emma," like a prayer — the only one she ever said. That helped her feel less like a fraud.

16

*T*HE ISSUE OF FORMAL THERAPY dissolved, de facto, in a tacit decision to have many "talks." After breakfast, one June morning, Katherine called Fran on the intercom to say that two cancellations gave her a free morning, and she'd enjoy holding the baby in her wheelchair, so why doesn't Fran take them to the park?

Fran fastened one of her long scarves in a sling around Katherine's left arm to secure a place for the baby. She put diapers, a blanket and lunch in a tote basket that slipped onto the back of the wheelchair.

While they were eating lunch, they watched two mothers sitting on a bench next to the wading pool. Every two minutes, the younger, plumper woman yelled, "No throwing sand, Robbie, no stones!" Her friend, a thin redhead, paid no attention to her two boys, although they were out-throwing Robbie. Katherine exchanged an amused look with Fran.

Soon all three boys wandered off behind their mothers to some large pine trees. After five minutes, the thin redhead got up, still talking to her friend, and moved quickly over to the tree where her four year old dangled by one arm and leg, about twelve feet from the ground. "My arm hurts, my leg hurts," he told her, and then he fell. But she was there to catch him.

Fran was amazed. "What did she hear? I thought she was impervious."

"I wasn't paying attention."

"What if she hadn't caught him! He could have been killed!"

"Kids are pretty tough. He'd probably only have broken a limb or two."

"His limbs — not the tree's!" Fran swept aside the pebbles she had laid along the edge of Caitlin's blanket. "Children need constant attention. All the time with Caitlin, I'm stretched, listening; it's as if I were to forget her, she'd come to harm. When I was little, they used to tease me about being absent-minded."

"So now you are always on guard not to daydream."

Fran stretched out on the grass, moved her arms and legs in the way children do when they are making snow angels. The baby slept on, rump up.

"I envy Cait. She can just relax. It makes me angry, sometimes, that I have to be so attentive."

Katherine watched Fran's index finger, almost touching a lady bug on its slow climb up a blade of grass. The grass blade tipped, ever so minutely, when the insect reached the top.

"Katherine, it's when you are most contented, on a summer day like today. The repetition of bees. We could be drugged by roses. It's all so lulling. Just when you've forgotten time, down comes the *big hand*."

"Was it like that the day your brother was killed?"

"I was gone that day, visiting a friend in the old neighborhood. It was the first time I was so far away from home. I remember being proud of a new bathing suit. I didn't feel like myself, but different. My legs were long wavy ribbon shapes under water. I remember feeling separate, peaceful. I remember thinking — these are my private thoughts. Like I was the dock and my thoughts were the boats I watched, nudging each other in the water without urgency. I can remember it all so well, because when we got home, Ruth Ann's mother was in the kitchen having coffee with my mother and we wanted to go outside and play; there was pounding on the door — Chris, a neighborhood boy, shouting Michael is drowned.

"And the next thing I remember is being at Martha's house, reading comic books when her mother comes in, puts me on her lap and says, 'Michael has gone to live with Jesus.' I knew that meant forever. The previous year my first cousin was killed in a car accident. I can remember thinking, at this cousin's funeral, I was glad to be in my family, because no one in my family would ever die. That was *before*, and all at once it was *after*. The biggest difference was, I think now, that when Michael died, I realized I had a past, and Michael was gone from it. In the future, would I lose someone else? But I think in a year or so I was thinking like a child again."

"You were back to living in the present."

"Until puberty. It's been after ever since. That second chance at childhood was an illusion, and too brief. Now I don't want to spend Cait's infancy carrying her up and down the stairs in a Snugli because I'm afraid I'll drop her. When she's old enough to climb trees, I want her to climb high. I'd like to be that redhead, and be able to listen for danger with only a small part of myself. Did you notice how she went right on with her conversation? Didn't miss a beat."

Katherine stirred restlessly, put her weight upon her right elbow, in an attempt to lift her hip. Fran looked guilty as she jumped up to help Katherine shift to another position. She extended and raised the leg rest.

"But, Fran," said Katherine, who now felt like taking the opposite view, "what if she hadn't gotten there in time? Her child is too young to be climbing trees like that. He has neither the judgment nor the coordination.''

"Well, my mother always said it was the happy-go-lucky mothers whose children survived with only scrapes. She was bitter, I think, about a neighbor, Mrs. Hill, who didn't keep an eye on her small children unless it suited her to do the ironing outside. And then she probably wanted to admire her begonias. She always used to say, 'Let the angels watch over them.' Her children, that is, not the begonias.''

Caitlin had been sleeping for over an hour. Katherine knew that the baby was turning night into day, and everyone would suffer for it. Why didn't Fran see that?

Katherine turned to her, an irritable lurch. The fresh air wasn't so pleasant when you had to sit; it was hot. "And better for the angels to watch over them than for the mothers to think they can control life and death if only they will be perfect enough! *Do* try to take that burden off yourself! You won't succeed.''

Fran blinked twice, and then turned away, hunching her shoulders a little. She began to gather together the remains of their picnic.

Katherine lowered her forehead into her palm. "Fran, I didn't mean that literally. What I meant to say is — common sense care is one thing; obsessive concern is another.'' That wasn't right either. Katherine felt, at once, both passive and agitated — as if she'd lost the state of grace and didn't quite care. But when Fran leaned over her to give her the sleeping baby, Katherine hugged her with the one good arm.

17

"HERE'S THE BABY. I need to work for a few hours," Fran told Alan.

"And I'm working on an article entitled, 'Baby's Bonding with the Modern Father,'" he said.

A smile might crack her face, and she thought, just don't be so *cheerful*, Alan. "I'm in a bad mood," she said. "Give her a bottle when she cries."

As she mixed her medium — slowly, so as not to get too much dammar varnish in the turpentine and linseed oil — she tried to decide how she felt. Katherine always told her she should pay more attention to her feelings. Katherine! Because of Katherine she felt — dull. No — hurt. No — more like angry! Katherine had been switching back and forth: First advocating maternal relaxation and then maternal vigilance, and then it was maternal abdication. Well, people had their moods. Not a comforting thought today.

Telling Katherine that her second chance at childhood ended at puberty: She hadn't known she thought that. A commonplace enough reflection, even if you hadn't lost a brother three years earlier. No, she was surprised because of her bitterness, her feeling of entrapment. Then — coming like a hologram — the memory of herself at eleven, or maybe twelve, out looking for Mark. Summer. Past nine o'clock because the streetlights were on already: "The dark is down," her mother used to say. Scared. Running — screams as she finds her breath, Mark, Mark, you little brat! Come home this minute! A stitch burns her side,acid her throat, forced air sears her lungs. She could kill her own dumb, slow, flesh and blood body. How she pushed her legs to go faster. Screams. Then the thought, "I'll punish you, God, I'll show you, I'll kill myself trying to keep them safe. Then you'll be happy." She digs her nails into her side where the pain is — root it out! A tickling deep inside her, a feeling of engorgement between her legs and moving up, deep, in the very center of her body: all her troubles came from the dumb, breakable, bloody (Let the clots come out!) body.

While she lived, once again, in the body she'd outgrown twenty years ago, her hand moved steadily over her painting,which grew in slow layers — vast spaces in a small area, only three discrete color shapes: A blue going in and out into white — perhaps a sky, an arching double line of mauved tan trying to reach what might be land in the middle distance, and upon it, an intermediate gray outcrop supporting the arch.

Deliberately, she intersected the bridge with a bold slate blue stroke, 1/4 inch wide. Because of the close values of the rest, this addition drew the eye, so further down she added the falling punctuation of an orange ellipse and a smaller one below, both shapes about to disappear, so transparent are they, into the river below.

That night she dreamed she was standing by the window: Outside, bobbing like helium balloons, were two intricately figured Chinese kites, birds with feathers of cerulean blue. The baby clung to her with one arm, and with the other, stretched to reach the kites. It occurred to Fran that she could get them for Caitlin if she went outside on the window ledge. She was immediately horrified at the thought of taking such a risk while holding a small baby. Then, while she was wondering what to do, she was seized by a wind from within the room — so strong that she rushed through the air and out the window. She reached for the baby to keep her from being blown away, and was horrified to discover that her hands were around the baby's neck.

Her shaking woke Alan, who mumbled, "What's wrong?"

"I had another nightmare. But I can't talk about it yet."

Just then the baby cried. Fran had weaned her, with mixed feelings, both loss and relief. No more stumbling out of bed, her breasts already spurting milk. The milk had made her feel uncontrolled, disorderly. It took over her body, annoyed her with its importunity. Yet no more sitting in the dark with her baby. When Caitlin used to suck, the milk had been a secret river, a shining band between them. Was it broken, was she guilty to want — less pressure? She was glad Alan could help at night, but she also wanted to keep Caitlin to herself. Would she ever again feel just one emotion at a time?

"Give her the bottle, Alan; I don't want to."

Fran rolled over on the far side of the bed, her back to them. Just as Alan was getting up to take the baby back to her crib, Fran turned and touched Cait's little finger.

When Alan came back, he pulled at his hair, making it stick out from his head in spikes. He looked comical, but she didn't feel like laughing.

"Want to . . . ?" he began.

"I have to work this out."

"By yourself, yes I know. But it makes me unhappy so see you like this. I just want you to know I think you're basically healthy."

She almost had to laugh. Alan, peering at her earnestly, asking her to accept his seal of approval and get on with her life.

"Katherine thinks you have a problem and so do I, or I wouldn't have urged you to start working with her. But I used to be your best friend.''

She noticed how he winced, and ran his fingers through his hair again. In any rehearsal of what he'd like to tell her, she knew he hadn't planned to say he needed her.

"Alan, I still feel close to you. It's complicated enough seeing Katherine about my problems. She wanted me to see Mrs. Neufrauw but I said no, I couldn't talk about my private life with someone I barely knew. Today she got mad after I told her some things about Michael's death, but I don't think she was just upset with *me* . . . Something she said made me feel hopeless at first, but not now, not even after that nightmare. Somehow the nightmare helped . . . She said I wouldn't succeed in keeping Cait safe.''

Alan had been sitting on the side of the bed as he rummaged about in the night table for a cigarette. He jumped up. "Shit! That's damn irresponsible of her. I wonder if she should be in practice. How much has her stroke affected her? You didn't need to hear that!''

"No, Alan, no . . . I don't understand yet, but I think that what she said triggered the dream I had, and I learned something important.''

He looked so frustrated, that she had to tell him her dream. Grateful that he didn't comment, she said, "This was an unblocking dream. Sometimes when I'm painting and I don't know where a shape should expand, or where a color should change into another, if I work on the problem from the top of my mind, I make a — jigsaw puzzle. It all fits, but it isn't alive. Then if I wander around, dreamy and vague, with a cup of coffee in my hand, I find myself back at the easel, brush in hand, with a solution that just grows onto the canvas. What Katherine said unsettled me so much, that something came loose and floated to the surface of my mind. I'm beginning to see it . . . what I have a right to fear.''

18

*F*RAN'S MOTHER WROTE Katherine from the Malley's summer home at
Logger's Loon lake in central Minnesota:

> *Dear Mrs. Morgan,*
>   *Or should I say Katherine — I feel that I know you*
> *through Fran and Alan. We've been wanting to meet you.*
> *Why don't you, if it is convenient, come with them for a*
> *week around the Fourth of July? Hope to see you soon.*
>   *Best wishes,*
>   *Margaret Malley*

Katherine could tell nothing from the note. Certainly to the point.
Not uncordial, but not overly friendly either. When Fran's parents had
come to see the baby on several occasions after her birth, Katherine
had been with a patient. She had thought it odd Fran couldn't persuade
them to stay for dinner.

Fran said, "Now, I hope you'll come. You could always stay with
Mitzi if you wanted a break from us, but we'd love to have you!"

Katherine saw that Fran meant just that, so they all went in her van,
like a family, she couldn't help thinking.

Two of Fran's younger brothers, Mark and Arthur, with their young
families, were already at the lake. It was obvious to Katherine that the
sprawling log cabin with the fieldstone foundation was Margaret's
place, rather than her husband's, and had been for thirty years. "I
learned how to do everything from plumbing to carpentry," her
hostess said over drinks their first evening. "Jim was always in the
Cities most of every summer. This vacation is typical — he goes to
every retired lawyers' convention in the country. You should have
seen that hill before I took the rocks out."

"Now, Mom, keep your sleeves rolled down," Mark said. "No one
wants to see your muscles."

Soon Fran, Alan, Katherine and the baby eased into the
"preestablished, every-summer rhythm," as Alan said: Each day
ended with long dinners of fish, hashbrowns, tomatoes, melons, wine
and talk and more wine. A pleasant hubbub, thought Katherine, as
conversations began, were sidetracked, reformed. Unfinished
sentences mixed together like the spaghetti. And nobody seemed to
care. The whole scene had an adult focus, Katherine noticed; the

children ate early and were encouraged to go out as soon as they were finished. Once, while outside the dining room window, Mark's two boys began crying over a creek turtle in a pail of sand and water, and Margaret dealt with them summarily: "We'll have no crying and whining, boys, enough!" Other sorts of noise didn't seem to bother her; all day the children banged in and out the screen door. For the grownups, it was fires, detective novels, and leisurely work — woodchopping, fishing, spreading clothes to dry on raspberry bushes.

Once, while Fran was reading, her six year old nephew lugged the baby (laboriously, his arms straining around her small chest) over to the minnow tank. "Cait likes the fishes to nibble on her toes." Fran, with a quickly-concealed start of alarm, laughed and put the baby back in her Portacrib. Katherine observed that Fran was a little proud of herself for acting like a robust, confident mother.

On the evening of the Fourth of July, Mark and Arthur built a beach bonfire. Their children ran back and forth from the kitchen to the picnic tables with the hot dogs, paper plates, buns and potato chips. Alan went into Fisherton to pick up his father-in-law at the small municipal airport. Fran was occupied with Caitlin. So Margaret pushed Katherine down the rutted gravel road to the beach.

"I don't know how you have adjusted so well to your stroke," she said. "I don't think I could do it myself." It was her first personal remark. Katherine couldn't turn to look at her, but she could imagine what Margaret's face would look like when doubtful. Vacated, perhaps? In the limbo of all determined optimists? Then Katherine felt ashamed of herself. She should recognize a compliment when she heard one. "Thank you, Margaret, it hasn't been easy, but if you had a stroke, I think you'd be a fighter."

Margaret didn't answer until she had maneuvered the wheelchair over a drainage ditch. Then she said, "Maybe, but what I would dread most is not being in control — I don't think I could live if I couldn't act."

She parked the wheelchair away from the picnic table, near some drift wood dividing the grass from the sand. The lake, Katherine thought, seemed high — as if at the top of a mountain, ringed by scalloped pines, a sloping cup within surrounding cranberry bogs. Margaret hesitated, and then sat down on a log facing Katherine. Her long, rather angular face wasn't vacant, no — she was literally biting her tongue! "I certainly hope I didn't offend you, Katherine."

No, she wasn't offended. Actually, it felt good — a woman her own age who knew about compromise and was honest enough to say she feared the final one. "No, you didn't. You understand something the young people don't," Katherine said. "I just begin to see how taking

65

action has always been such a *muscular* thing for me; I used to think I spent my working hours, at least, using my mind. Now I see I was fooling myself. Finding solutions to my problems, the problems of my patients, was much more like going to the refrigerator when you didn't know what you wanted to eat. You know — how you stand there in a brown study, and then all of a sudden your hand comes back with something in it.''

Margaret smiled, and then she laughed. A deep chuckle, matching her voice. She rose to her feet, pulled her plaid shirt down. I used to be that tall, Katherine thought. ''Well, I've spent half my life, it seems,'' Margaret said, ''coming back to the table with something in my hand. It didn't matter how many we had for dinner — four more, or . . . one less.''

''Fran told me that you lost a son many years ago.'' Katherine drew in a breath. Had she misunderstood, or presumed too much on their first real talk?

But Margaret only sat down again, after a quick glance over to the picnic table. She looked at Katherine and nodded her head. ''He died shortly before his fifth birthday. He would have been twenty-nine years old this year.'' A simple and direct answer. She pushed her fingers along her temples, through her short gray hair. ''Sometimes I go for days without thinking of him.''

''It's very hard, and you don't forget,'' Katherine said, and had an impulse to tell Margaret about Emma. But no, she hadn't told Fran . . .

''It was more difficult at first until I learned not to think of him in a way that hurt. You just have to keep going — which I did.''

''All those demands from your large family — everyone needing pieces of you — I wonder if it is somewhat the same for me, to a less personal degree, with my patients? Did you ever think that you hadn't much more to give? When you were younger did you want to be left alone?''

''Oh, I fell asleep, dog-tired, every night at nine. But no, I've always been grateful that I didn't have too much time to brood. I wasn't born a brooder, and I didn't want to turn into one.''

''Ah, for me, there's much time to brood now when I'm waiting for other people's help — getting back to what you said before about dreading inactivity — but brood, that's a nice word in a way, full of warmth and caring. Now that I can't just get up and get what I want anytime I'm hungry or thirsty, I brood a little. At those times I send my spirit to the well, though sometimes the bucket comes back empty.''

''I don't quite understand what you mean, unless it's finding that your disability isn't entirely a bad thing for you? The way you talk reminds me of Alan.''

Margaret's eyes were very blue, and Katherine thought of Fran. "I guess I meant to say my disability is an opportunity, but one I don't always use very well.''

"Send your spirit to the well . . . Are you religious?''

Was she religious? How to tell Margaret, who had snorted about Mark's wife's "communion with nature," last Sunday when the family was expected to go to mass, that she felt religious about wind, water, and all growth? "Yes, I'm religious. As a psychologist, I think more about the spirit than the psyche.''

"Speaking of spirits, let me get us some wine cooler. I'll be right back.''

Katherine watched Margaret take the hill in several long strides. (How many women her age wore blue jeans so well?) She was willing to bet that Margaret would find something to do in the kitchen. This sort of conversation was not her style.

But no, Margaret was back in just a few minutes with the drinks and a cheese tray. "I guess I'm an old fashioned Catholic," Margaret said, "because for me, the Holy Spirit is the third person of the Blessed Trinity. Alan, as you may have noticed, is always getting excited about some new idea, and a year or so ago he and Fran took me to one of those charismatic meetings. Well, I was never so uncomfortable in my life, wondering who would feel the spirit next. The lady next to me jumped up out of her seat with tears streaming down her face, and started talking pig Latin, or some such gibberish. It made me dizzy. Some of those people, with their hair all over, looked like they'd gotten caught in an electric fan.''

"Caught in what?" Fran, wearing a sleeping Caitlin in the Snugli, stepped gingerly, first one foot, then another down the last stretch of eroded path.

"I was telling Katherine about that fool spirit meeting you took me to.''

Fran grinned — a little teasing there? — if so, a new side to her. "Alan called; Dad's plane is late. He says we should go ahead and eat whenever we want.''

"Oh, let's stay over here," Margaret said. "Let the kids and their parents have the table.'' She went over to the picnic table and filled a plate for Katherine, and then returned with two more for Fran and herself.

Fran folded several thick towels into a basket, and then unzipped the Snugli, slowly drawing Caitlin out so as not to wake her. She laid the baby inside, covering her with a cotton sheet and some mosquito netting. Both women watched as she put the basket fifteen feet away under a large blue spruce.

"That's real progress, Fran. When that baby was first born, you never put her down," Margaret said.

Katherine looked sharply at Margaret. Had Fran told her mother she was in therapy? No, surely not — because Fran frowned, and pursed her lips at Katherine. Katherine shook her head, and put one finger on her mouth.

Margaret misinterpreted. "Oh, she'll sleep very well out here. And this way my daughter won't be running up the hill every few minutes to check on her."

Was Margaret consciously baiting Fran? Of course not. Why would she be smiling at her with such obvious affection? She just doesn't know what Fran has been going through, Katherine decided. Because Fran hasn't told her? Because she doesn't want to know?

Fran said, "When do we begin the fireworks?"

"Oh, not until after nine, when it gets dark. *You* know! Katherine, Fran was just terrified of fireworks when she was as old as seven or eight."

"Oh, many children are," Katherine said.

"And many are not. But my little mouse here would come and hide on my lap."

"Did anyone remember to get sparklers for the four monsters over there?" Fran asked. The cousins were running up and down the pier, cheering as the first stars appeared. The last peach cloud had faded into blue behind the black rim of fir trees at the other end of the lake.

"I did," said Mark, who was taking the coffee around, "and Arthur bought the fireworks in Decatur. How many years have we been doing this? I remember, when we were young, the Fourth of July made Frances really fierce. Cress and I used to run around the beach, and she always thought we were going to get hit when Dad, or Uncle Dick set the rockets off. She kept after Arthur, Bill and Jenny to wear shoes because of hot sparkler sticks."

"Fran was responsible — at least when she knew what was going on around her," Margaret said. "Give me some more coffee, Mark, or I'll never stay awake."

Fran, her bare feet stretched toward the lake, had been making a pattern with a stick in the wet sand. She dug her stick in, and half-turned toward her mother. "What do you mean — when I knew what was going on around me?"

"Oh, you were always drawing something. And you concentrated so hard that when anyone spoke to you, you didn't even hear."

"I heard a lot more, and I knew a lot more than you ever gave me credit for." Fran stood on her tiptoes, and for a moment Katherine thought that she was going to shake both fists, but instead she clasped her hands behind her head and arched her body in a yawn. In what ethnology tome, wondered Katherine, did I read about a yawn being a sign of repressed anger?

"Let's change the subject," Fran said. "Mark, remember how the Smothers Brothers used to say, 'Mother always loved you best'?"

Everyone laughed. Margaret, who had moved to a lounge chair, patted the cushion: "Come, sit next to your old mother for old times sake, mouse."

The children were drawing on the dark with their sparklers, when Alan arrived with his father-in-law. While some men would enjoy a boisterous demonstration of affection by their family, Jim Malley seemed the sort of person who chose to arrive unnoticed in dim light. Not tall, but broad — a geriatric jogger if I ever saw one, Katherine thought. A firm handshake, so pleased to have you here, and so forth. "Fran, you're looking well," he said and bent to put his arm around her. "How's the work going?" Fran, who had been sitting on the edge of her mother's chair, jumped up to return his embrace. She visibly relaxed. "I have one canvas in the boathouse, but it's too dark to show you tonight."

Alan, singing the Star Spangled Banner, came down to the beach with more beer, soda, mosquito spray and a few blankets against the beginning of a chill.

"I'd better put Caitlin back into the Snugli," said Fran.

Alan tucked a light blanket around Katherine's legs. "Need a sweater?"

"No, dear, thanks." Alan seemed well-established in Fran's family. Did he feel closer to them than to his own folks? Not particularly, Katherine decided. Despite his efforts to keep every part lively, he was the sort of person who, inside himself, was not easily at home outside his own home — which was her home. A real contradiction there . . .

The children now sat quietly in the rowboat, still tied to the pier. "Ooo aah ooh aah ooo aah oooo," they chorused as minute colored lights popped low against the horizon fifteen miles away in Fisherton. "Oooh ah chaddy waddy bing bang, let's sound like that old song of Daddy's," said Mark's oldest boy.

"Can't impress these kids with anything nowadays," Alan said, and he chuckled.

"But they wouldn't trade coming to the lake for all the big bangs at the state capitol either," Mark replied. "It was the same for us — right Fran?"

Fran, slumped back against Alan with the sleeping weight of Cait, nodded a drowsy yes. Katherine felt a little chilly, and she wished she'd told Alan to fetch her sweater when he asked. Now he looked too comfortable to disturb. So she was glad when Mark put another log on the fire. Then Margaret, without saying a word, put a beach towel around Katherine's shoulders. Before Katherine could thank her, she went around to the other side of the fire to sit next to her husband.

Arthur called, "You kids get out of the boat now; we're going to start the rockets." A spurt of a match, then going up, a hiss and then, at the downward arch, blue and yellow sparks, brief — like a bud, and a splash. The next one went a little higher, ripping till it paused, almost ten o 'clock to the pier, red — a half-opened flower. Then so many opened above her raining down their harmless fire, that her neck grew tired from holding her head back. On either side of their clearing, were woods — a solid wall, broken only by the neon tracery of fireflies. So she turned instead to the water. Except for the reflection of their campfire, she would need to take the lake — now a black hole — on faith.

19

WHEN THEY RETURNED to Minneapolis, Katherine, because she wanted to be more professional, decided that Fran should come to her office for their work. Yet she was of two minds. The park, with its prosaic dangers, was not necessarily a bad place for analysis. Jung himself had written about synchronicity: Didn't Fran's emotion conjure up a child falling from a tree? Many analysts would welcome such visual aids! But her own emotions in the park — she felt embarrassed to remember — had overflowed the situation. And now that she knew more about Fran's family, she felt, in a complex way, that she needed her desk, her books and papers, close at hand.

"Your parents have such a great capacity for enjoyment."

Fran nodded as if that was what people always said. She shifted her lounge chair to face the garden-side wall of windows. Katherine did the same to her wheelchair, and thought that they must look more like two passengers on an ocean liner than analyst and analysand.

"What do you remember about your mother right after your brother drowned?"

"I remember the next morning. After she got out the cereal and the bowls for breakfast, she sat down at the table and cried into her hands. I don't remember her crying again after that."

"Was she changed toward you — more protective?"

"Only that once when she ran across the street to take me from the apple orchard."

"Did you ever ask her how she coped — what kept her going?"

The light was lower now, in Fran's eyes. She adjusted the chair higher. Rather than turning to look at me, Katherine thought, Fran is very good at avoiding – her mother at the lake, and now me . . .

"She said the only thing that saved her was having to care for Mark and me. And her faith."

"And she went on to have four more children."

"I don't see how she could have done that. But then, having only one child makes me feel vulnerable. It's very irrational."

"And people in your family are not supposed to be irrational. Am I right?"

"Yes. My mother couldn't stand to hear us cry or complain. She'd always say – 'No use crying over spilt milk.' or – 'Less said, sooner mended.'"

"Your parents didn't say much about Michael's death."

"My mother also said, 'No use talking about something you can't do anything about.' But Mark had nightmares and cried when he heard sirens, and banged his head against the wall, and ground his teeth as he slept. I was too old when Michael died to be afraid of sirens. I remember thinking that nobody noticed how brave I was. And about Mark — when I was young, I never connected Michael's death to anything Mark did as a three year old child. It may seem odd to you, but in my family we just say, 'Oh, that's the way so-and-so is — always has been high strung,' or something of that sort. But then when I took a psychology course my freshman year in college, I wondered if Mark's stomachaches were connected to Michael's death. Still I thought it was strange to be thinking about something that had happened ten years ago. My family always said I was too serious. So I wanted to be like my mother, who enjoyed life.''

"Even though she lost a son, she enjoyed life.''

"That's the way it should be! Nothing could bring him back. My mother understood that because she was a grownup when it happened. Oh, what an obvious thing to say . . . ''

"Nothing is obvious. I think that's what you felt at eight — that it was easier for her because she was older and more powerful.''

"Yes! And she herself had a happy childhood. She hadn't lost an older brother, like Mark did. Mark missed Mike so, but nobody ever explained a thing to him. Maybe because he was so little when it happened.''

"Nobody ever explained his death to you?''

"They said it was God's will.''

"What did Jesus say — 'Even the little that you have shall be taken away'?"

"Oh, that's a hard thing to say. I don't think he . . . No, that saying was connected to the parable of the talents. The servant who buried his had it taken away.''

"Don't you think that we all bury valuable parts of ourselves? Maybe we bury those aspects of the self because we are trying to protect something else even more precious to us? You know Fran, you come from a good family. And when your brother died, your parents, who are tough, but loving people, wanted to preserve the warmth and security of your family atmosphere. What's wrong with that?''

"I think you missed the tension.'' Fran glanced at Katherine as if she were afraid she'd been tactless. Then she explained. "It's different now that my Dad's retired and we're all grown. The family's much more relaxed. But we still have a tendency to kick at the most minute physical restrictions. Did you see how my mother turned the cabin upside down when she couldn't find her car keys? We all hate to lose things. I'm like that but, like her, I usually hide it." Fran mimed yanking at her hair. "Alan calls it, 'thin air phobia.' He says I'm afraid things will vanish out of perversity. He's right."

Katherine chuckled, and then said, "That's a very important insight, Fran, and I'll get back to it in a bit . . . " She was quiet for a few moments. "I did notice one sign of tension. At the cottage, every evening was a special occasion, and that's normal on a vacation — but I wonder about the feelings I sensed . . . Your family life seems, how shall say it — heightened!"

"Katherine, I think we go from celebration to celebration — every family meal — as if to say, 'Thank God we're all still here. ' "

Katherine felt a strong exasperated fondness for Fran, and — she had to face it — a professional disappointment. Until Fran sounded so, so — naively egotistical, the session seemed to be going well. Celebration to celebration, indeed! She'd thought that Fran herself had, in the last half hour, begun to see the sort of emotional repression that caused Mark's symptoms. Surely, she should have connected her own symptoms, not to Michael's death, but to the repression of Michael's death? Katherine looked at Fran's smooth skin, clear eyes, and well-tended hair. She wanted to shake her. She knew Fran had suffered, was suffering. It was, of course, Katherine's own projection. She tried to pull it back. Her notebook, resting on her knee, was empty save for a large circle. She bore down on her fine flair marker and the circle spiraled inward. When she reached the center, she said, "Look, Fran, remember the time I was angry with you in the park? I'm irritated again, and it's the same stimulus. Let me think this through out loud — as unwise as that might be. It's at least partly my problem, but — well, damn, I keep thinking you're relentlessly romantic. You think of your family as gallant — eat, drink and be merry for tomorrow we die. Perhaps you think that together you face death, having experienced it together. But you never were encouraged to *feel* it! No one ever said that it was all right to feel bad! After the tragedy, everything was under control, and now you feel you should be able to guard your child's life, prevent her death. Most of us just do the best we can."

Fran half rose out of her chair as she spun around to face Katherine. "Again you seem to say it's all fate! You're supposed to build my confidence. As a psychologist, you're depressing!"

Katherine suddenly realized what she has needed to tell her. "It's the opposite of depressing. It's freeing. Jung said . . . Hand me that book." Katherine turned the pages of large volume, a clumsy search with one hand, until she found a passage that she read slowly, and with emphasis: " 'If we do not partially succumb (to the evil), none of this apparent evil enters into us and no regeneration or healing can

73

take place.' "

"Fran, there's something Faustian in your refusal to relax. By your vigilance, you think you can do what your mother didn't do. *Your* child will live! *Allow* the knowledge of Caitlin's inevitable death — some time, some place. Her death is her own and it has much less to do with you than you think. You're her mother; you wish her all good, but you're not God."

Quite a speech and all wrong, totally wrong. The insights belonged to her, not to Fran. What a fiasco, especially when she had decided from the beginning not to be so directive. Katherine thought, and not for the first time, that a wheelchair was most inconvenient when she'd like to walk away, pretend to shuffle some papers on her desk. She wished she smoked. Fran was looking straight out the window. Hurt? Over-load? It was hard to tell.

20

AFTER A SESSION with Katherine, Fran was often glad to slip away. Such a jumble of emotions! As in political fights, reasons didn't matter. As soon as you saw one argument clearly, in all fairness, you had to see the opposite: claims nestled one within the other, like Chinese boxes. If you cared, you didn't feel like opening boxes, you felt like smashing them. What was the point in allowing herself to "feel bad"? Feelings were disorderly.

Katherine was always glad to find emotions and call them reasons — as if unearthing Fran's childhood marbles from the mud, and calling them jewels. So, Fran was to allow herself to "feel bad"? She'd rather "work good." Even good feelings, sooner or later, coiled under her ribs into anger.

Like caring. Fran knew her family thought she was apolitical when she was just the opposite. She cared too much about lead emissions from gasoline (retarded children), nuclear weapons (the death of all children). Caring made her want to erase smug smiles with a scream. But she didn't want to be angry with death. That would be mad. Was she angry with Katherine, who wanted her to feel something, something about death? No. She even felt detached from the "relentlessly romantic" girl. Woman. She couldn't bear to think about these things. She couldn't bear to be chaotic.

Neither did she like to talk about her paintings. Criticism seemed silly — as if giving an after-the-fact importance to something. Documentation was for those who doubted.

What was important? Order and deft movements, her brush an extension of her hand. Beginning her current painting, she had laid down a color, with just a groping toward form. Then she was deeply satisfied to see the first closure: a greyed-vermilion plane rising up behind a green cloud. She saw the hidden geometry, the bones, the diagonal planes converging toward the top and bottom, where they joined in a diamond floating back into the picture plane. The diamond remained attached, held in tension by the square that contained it. Then it receded so steeply, the upper corner was cut off.

Fran remembered that Katherine (who seemed so far away, in her own world, busily tending paper flowers in a glass of water) had been excited about this painting. Like Alan, Katherine responded to form and color in a literary way. Katherine had said, "Where did that image come from!"

Fran didn't want to know where from. It had come and that was enough. But Katherine had nodded, and said, "The square or diamond is satisfying. Of course. Jung spoke about the quaternities: Intellect needs emotion. Sensation needs intuition. You are a person who has taken refuge in what you can make, in what you can touch. Maybe, maybe, the wind is a compensation. You need your heels off the ground for a while? Maybe?

"It's a tricky technical illusion," Fran had said, and her fingers brushed the glazed surface of the canvas. Must Katherine always bring psychology in? "It seems I can almost touch this corner of the diamond . . . but only because the other has receded."

"That's what I was trying to say," Katherine had replied.

It was easier to listen to Katherine when emotions were red and green, and moved away from you just as you thought you'd caught them. She was standing on tiptoe, and it all began to make some sense.

21

ALAN'S DESK FACED the south window overlooking the backyard. Each morning after breakfast, he watched Fran bump down the stairs with the buggy or stroller, and then go back in for Caitlin. Sometimes she would sit on the back steps for a half an hour or so before leaving. Then he would watch them go out the gate. He could see them still as they stood at the crossing, but lost sight of them as they turned the corner toward the park. He felt he had lost the ability to imagine what anyone was like.

When he was still at the U., he used to play "true story" with the other editors of the *Minnesota Beacon*, their literary magazine, in the Gopher Hole after games. Much of their conjecture involved sexual preference, with references to Oscar Wilde, and much of it involved, Alan thought now, the most naive sort of projection: "I think that grey-haired man over there, the one with the stooped back and inky fingers, is a former Albanian foreign exchange student from cold war years, who has returned on a visa, as a well-known eastern block poet. He will try to impress Dr. Ellis, but she will, after several late night drinks, put her long blond hair back into a French twist, and tell him, 'Sorry – the feeling is gone, Aldo.'"

"Been reading too much Ian Fleming lately, Alan?" Addison Hazel, who carried around a copy of *Ullyses*, had smiled into his glass of beer as he tapped the end of his English Oval upon the table.

Alan could have swallowed his tongue. "Keep your own counsel, boy," said Nona, and — "Don't let the tail wag the dog." She also said, "If someone gets the best of you, don't let on."

"Oh," said Alan, "You should try a few spy stories too, Addison. You've been carrying that copy of *Ullyses* around for a long time now. All Joyce and no joy makes a dull boy." Not bad. And, 15 years later, Alan felt he had gotten even better at red-penciling other people's remarks, other people's text.

His junior year he'd met Fran, who couldn't be bothered accommodating herself to ego games. Nona — if she'd ever said more to Fran than, "I suppose your people don't make pesto" — should have admired Fran's indifference. If she didn't see that Fran was unaware there *was* a game, she might think that Fran maneuvered people into playing by her rules — something Nona would enjoy immensely. Nona would like hearing how Fran told off the head of the art department. Fran and Nona should be friends.

But how to reconcile the contained, confident Frances, her eye-on-the-canvas simplicity, with this worried mother, tucking in Caitlin as if her very life depended on a snug blanket? The old Frances seldom did anything she didn't want to do. No, he hadn't progressed much beyond "true story." Anyone's real story would be guesswork, and, even if they told you — a facade.

He sat at his desk, but he couldn't write. He sharpened a pencil to avoid his typewriter, and his short story, which was so close to being finished. But Peter, who once seemed so vividly flexible, now seemed merely indecisive. How could he make Peter surprising? No, he couldn't plan a surprise. Yet a phrase from a novel by Pamela Hansford Johnson kept running through his head: "the appearance of subtlety, when a character says one thing, and then proceeds to do precisely the opposite." It was just the sort of tone he had wanted for his own work. But now he thought of "appearance" as diddling about with the surface, fiddling with mannerisms. Unless you understood the emotions. What was Peter's problem? Why couldn't that man get close to women?

Why couldn't *he* get closer to Fran? He thought of all the times he had entered the sunny places of her childhood story (chunks of bread and cheese at sunrise for canoe rides over fog-filled lakes). He'd hoped that, sometime, they'd take a trip together into the stagnant marsh backwash. And perhaps she'd turn to him one day and say, "No one knows me like you do." Was that what he wanted? He wanted to talk about her secrets, no — her inner being. He hadn't realized how much he still believed in souls.

All his life he'd had attacks of loneliness, times when he decided that, after all, no one could know another person — really. But he'd always recover when he had a "great conversation." "Bull sessions in the college dorm," his father used to say with some contempt — some curiosity too. Before Alan's birth, his father had wanted to go to college. Of that old ambition, all that remained was a dislike of young marriages — never mind that Alan and Fran had entered their thirties in some stability, after more than a decade together. Leo and Nona were united in their disregard of Fran.

Now, Alan was awakened by Frances nightly as she tried to surface from her nightmares, bathed in sweat and shivering. She no longer gave him her dreams. He'd told her they were "incredibly interesting!" "Interesting to you, maybe — terrible for me!" said Fran. He now thought he made a big mistake confiding his study of dreams to her — dreams with a wind motif. "You writers will *use* anything!" she cried.

She still wore the yellow crinkle crepe nightgown from her pregnancy. And now, despite frequent washing, it smelled of sour milk. Once she rebuffed him, when he tried to hold her close, and got up to wake the baby instead. He was hurt. Sometimes she hugged him, as if she'd like to burrow into his body, but she wouldn't talk. She saved herself for Katherine. At times he felt lonely, but not resentful. He admitted that Frances would never have *chosen* to reveal herself to anyone — even to herself.

What was it like to *be* Frances? What was it like to be a woman? He'd asked Katherine that one day when they were sitting at her table — he'd started coming over for a cup of coffee after he finished three hours at his desk. Ostensibly, he came to fix Katherine's lunch. (She made a sandwich or a salad, slowly, by herself, but, when she had only one hour between sessions, it didn't give her much time to relax.)

Katherine had gotten a secretive-amused look upon her face. "Do you have a lifetime? When you are an older woman, you think you know what it is like to be a younger woman. But that is only because everything is simplified from a distance — all those untidy emotions smoothed over."

"When do you think you know what it is like to be an older woman . . . when you are an *old* woman"

He had meant to be funny, but she only smiled. "Oh, Alan, maybe this is a blessing after all, but nothing is smoothed over any more. I am humbled that much of my serenity, stability, was nothing more than my rude good health."

Alan had his health, but he didn't always have his work. Sometimes it was blown away — by what? By the over-drive of his own mind? Piling up voices and images until — to borrow a metaphor from Leo — his engine was flooded. Crank, crank, crank, but it just wouldn't turn over. Alan got up from his desk, and then sat down again. He thought of Fran going out the gate, and he wrote the words: "She seemed to be_____, but she was really_____" at the top of a blank sheet of legal-sized yellow paper. It was an unblocking exercise from a long-ago writers' workshop. He was supposed to start free-associating. But his legs, his buttocks, felt stiff. Although he had slept eight hours, a part of him had worked at watching himself sleep — like an irritable night nurse. All night long he had written on his chart: "not deep enough" or — "too shallow." He stretched, and bent to touch his toes. Maybe he shouldn't start his writing exercise with Fran. What did Katherine do when she felt tense? The thought made him a little uncomfortable — as if he were wondering about the private physical life of his mother. He remembered a drama class he'd taken his senior year. "Let your body tell you how you feel," said the instructor.

I am Katherine, Alan thought, and stooped over. No — that was an old woman. Katherine was a listing-over-to-one side. Center of gravity is no longer a plumb line. A skewed twisting, a cork screw, the left arm drawn in spasmodically to the waist, the hand trying to become a claw. No — a resistance. Think wing! Lift the head, lift the head, roll to the right side, the left. Resistance — terrible strain. The right side protests — a pain in the ribs that sears her — all the way to her calf. Up on the knees — at first like a two legged stool — no feeling on the left side, and yet she doesn't fall. Rocking forward, backward — returning her to the first rocking, enclosed sea. ("It's all in the inner ear — the balance. She has to reclaim her *whole* body," the therapist had said.) Tears in her eyes. But the body wants to lie. Lie down. Under the skin, the blood would spread and stain, leaving those bruises of the bed-ridden. So she sits — gripping with her right hand, tensing her back muscles. And that is hard enough. The body would sit forever and the thighs would flatten — flaccid — to the pillow. Sharp pelvis bones would erode the skin. She could die in her chair, chair ridden, so she begins — to stand. At first, bent over, then little by little, straightening, and one step, and two. Katherine would move toward Fran.

And now he must move into his wife. But how? He wrote, " Her head is turning — her eyes never rest on her painting for longer than a brush stroke before lighting again on Caitlin. Her back bends, stubborn, over the drawing pad. Her smooth fingers, with their impossibly narrow first joints, wide spatulate thumb (No — that is Alan seeing.), an aching in the knuckles as she stretches a canvas — the first one since Caitlin. (No — that is Alan, trying to think like Frances.)"

He recalled how he had found Fran yesterday morning — sleeping on the floor next to the baby's crib, a bottle, half full of milk, dripping slowly into her hand. He lay down on the floor, assumed Fran's posture: A heaviness, a sinking down, a thin thread following, attached to the hook of her finger and — plummeting — like a fishing line — then, an obstacle, she's pulled up short — halfway between the surface and the bottom — dangling on a short line, and — floating above her on the surface — the loose line above the sinker, threaded through the eye of a bobber, bright blue — rocked by a cry — deep red, a rapid tugging on the line — a buoy, a bottle — her wrist, three drops, bluey white.

Off shore — the large white island, once enclosing them both, recedes, disappears. She, much smaller, drifts into the shallows, is pulled up, is beached, wet, and will be damp forever. Caitlin's cries are damp and pull her up. The cries are dangerous, to stop them, she stares into the baby's eyes. If the baby will look back, the island will form again, saving them both with its milky whiteness – no prints on the sand but theirs.

It felt very, very right. And he'd forgotten to write it down! But he didn't write like that. His imaginary world was solidly populated with *things*: He pictured the home of Fran's parents: *The Magic Mountain* on the coffee table next to the hand-tied trout flies. Due to her background, Fran had a wounded innocence. Privileged in everything but a sense of immunity to death. What would it be like to be conscious, much of the time, that your child was living in danger? It was only the truth, but what would it be like without most people's comfortable fictions? He mustn't exaggerate. Fran was not an existential tragedy queen. She hadn't the temperament for it. No – the curious thing was – she had a happy disposition, one inclined to ease. Unlike him, she worked steadily without compulsion. Until Caitlin, she had seldom seemed anxious.

He thought of his own parents' home: the Sears catalog on the table next to the greasy Pontiac alternator. (His Dad had salvaged all their cars.) In contrast to Fran's family life, he'd grown up with people who had little expectation of joy, and who, therefore, were seldom disappointed. Because of this, Alan thought, he was now an adult who *allowed* himself to clown. "Don't foam off at the mouth, boy," his father always said.

His playwriting class in college didn't teach him that the play could write itself. He had the set and he had the characters. His thin, dream-deprived sleep had even given him a waking dream. (He'd better record the island dream before he lost it.) But – something was missing. The characters didn't do anything. Actually, there was only one character – the God-author, who sat around thinking the characters into being, and who sometimes ran down on small change – like a magic finger bed at the Interstate 694 Hideaway.

His dad had gone to the Interstate Hideaway after his mom took little Alan to the emergency room, after his dad had taken his strap to little ten year old Alan and the buckle scratched his cornea. They'd had a big fight about that. "Goddammit, I'm no child abuser and I'm not going to have our family business in the files of some poker-assed lady from the social services."

"He has to have attention, Leo!"

"I tell you it's just a scratch on the eyeball – I had the same thing trimming the hedge – the doc didn't do nothing for me but put a little patch over the eye."

"He put in some disinfectant! He gave you a shot!"

"All right, all right – so go – I'm no monster, but keep your trap shut! That goes for you, boy."

81

Nona had been clucking in the background. "You're right, you're right, but get that boy to the hospital." It was one of the few times she half-way sided with his mom over his dad.

He got the patch, the disinfectant, and the shot as predicted. His mom told the doctor — "Scratched while trimming the hedge," in a strangled sort of voice. It was early December and the doctor gave her a funny look.

"His father live at home?" he asked.

"Not at the present," she said, and it was true. He'd already left for the Hideaway.

He'd never forgot that night. After she brought him home from the hospital she told his grandmother to go back downstairs; they had to be alone. Nona backed out of the door — for once without a saying. Then his mother poured herself a large drink of his dad's whiskey. She got him a coke from his grandma's supply, and told him to sit down, there was something important she had to say. "I swear to you if he ever lays another hand on you again, I'm going straight back to that doctor, and the social services too." Then she started crying, and crying, calling him "her little man." He wondered why he had to become her little man first for her to be strong. Why hadn't it been the bruises? What was it made her — finally — brave enough to take his side? Nona, who pretended to take his side, was worse than his mother. "I hate you all," he told his mother. And she cried worse than before. "If I don't have you, little man, I don't have anyone." And she told him things about his father, how his father never bothered to wash or please her. After a while he stuck his fingers in his ears, but, at the look on her face, his face sort of collapsed too, and then he was sitting on her lap, and she was kissing his patch and saying sorry, God knows how I'm sorry, and I'll make it up to you. He wanted to push her away and he wanted to hug her tight. Her face was too damp. She was too close. Was that what it was like to be a woman?

22

BY FALL, KATHERINE could walk a few steps with Fran and the quad cane. Fran, her arm around Katherine's waist, could feel the trembling, the tauntness of her determination. Caitlin was almost eight months old, and she, or Fran, graduated from the Snugli. As she carried the baby, Fran told Katherine that her arms felt stronger — just like Katherine's legs — and she was not so afraid of stairs. "The next time I have a dream that Cait is tumbling down a flight of stairs, I think I'll stop the dream and say, Look here, my child is getting almost old enough to crawl up and down the stairs by herself. This nonsense has got to stop!"

"It will be exhilarating for you to become more matter of fact — with Caitlin and even with your dreams, " Katherine said. She commented that her sister, who has been living in Zurich almost forty years, had raised her children in a no-nonsense European fashion. "We Americans tend to hover. We have this phobia about colds. Our poor little babies are buried in all those summer clothes, and they never get any fresh air from November to April."

Fran, who wanted to be a no-nonsense mother, decided to take Caitlin out in her snow suit for an airing in the buggy one morning in early November. She knew Alan watched from his window as she bumped the buggy down the back steps. Her confident adjustments of blanket and bottle, her brisk steps — all probably fooled him into thinking she was almost cured. Or maybe he wasn't fooled. Now she could take the baby up and down the stairs without putting her in the Snugli, but when she went out the door, she was afraid and never ceased to be afraid. What if, on an impulse, she were to leave the buggy in the middle of a busy intersection? What if she fainted? But she thought of Katherine, how she said, 'Slow and easy and I'll get there."

The park was almost empty except for an elderly couple taking a slow turn around the lake. Fran followed them, scuffling box elder leaves underfoot. The buggy creaked. A raucous flock of crows fought overhead in an oak. It was a day to feel at one, removed, peacefully detached, from everything, everyone. The sun, just a pale disk behind low clouds, hazy light, last week's snow flurries forgotten in this shallow, out-of-season mildness.

When she had completed the circle, and come back to the fork in the path where she had started, Fran rested on the only bench over a small rise, sloping down into the water. She could park the buggy while Caitlin slept. The lake, all bloom long skimmed from shore, looked cleansed, as if in April, after weeks of rain. The mirror of water caught the sun as it moved forward out of the clouds. It was almost warm. She loosened her scarf and tilted her face backward toward the sky, her fingers laced together behind her neck. Then she tucked her legs sideways on the bench, rested her head on her arm.

The elderly woman's scream woke her. "Joe! That baby buggy's rolling into the lake!" Fran almost knocked the old man over as she ran past him down the hill. Then the shock of icy water on her feet and legs. Caitlin's outraged cries — Fran herself must have splashed water into the baby's face in her haste to stop the buggy before it rolled deeper. When she stopped it, the water came half-way up the wheels.

The old man called from shore, "The baby's all right, isn't it! Just a scare. Mother, this little woman is all wet — do we have a blanket in the trunk?"

Fran lifted Caitlin, who immediately stopped crying. Then she turned away from the mired buggy toward the bank, raising her feet in slow motion, into marl with every step — like a nightmare when you cannot move. As if she were someone else, she heard each step squish and suck.

The old woman held her arms out: "Here, dear, let me hold the baby while you go back for the buggy."

"No, I'm going to leave it there. I can't take her home, I can't. My husband will have to . . . " How had it happened? Had she herself kicked the buggy with her foot while she slept? What if the old couple hadn't come? She would have slept while Caitlin drowned.

The old man came back with a blanket, and put it around her shoulders.

"There, there," said his wife, patting Fran's arm. "Your baby is just fine." And, in a lower voice to her husband: "She doesn't want to get the buggy, but you shouldn't either . . . We'll drive them home, get her husband. Shock."

On either side, the old couple led her to their car, a stately but ancient Chrysler. In her confusion she gave the address of her childhood, then corrected herself, felt sure that she had transposed two numbers, but which two?

She tried to remember Katherine's address, but could only recall the street. "Surely, I'll recognize the house," she said, and laughed so hard she shook the baby, and the baby started to cry, or she did . . . The old man was looking at his wife, so she tried to stop the crying.

"No harm done, no harm done — unless you take a cold," said the old woman. "Why, the baby would have slept right through it except for all the commotion."

"Mother," the old man said in a warning voice.

No one made any commotion at all when she "saved" Mark from drowning. Hadn't thought about that in years: Mark in his good suit, and she in her best dress — the one she sacrificed to the pond — all to save Mark. But her mother said, "Oh Frances, it was bad enough to have him get wet and muddy, but now look at you!" Then she felt embarrassed to say that she'd gone in to save him. At nine years old! She knew the pond was two feet shallow. It would have been so fine if — really — she had saved him.

By the time that Alan came back with the buggy, Fran had gone to bed. To avoid talking, she pretended to be sleeping. But soon she was asleep, and, as if lying in wait for her, within a thicket of bare trees, the dream rose up, voices first, a procession through the woods. It was Cress and Arthur, then Bill and Mark. Bringing up the rear was little Jenny. Someone held her hand, and it was — Michael. Only Michael and Jenny were free of the burden the others carried. It was a box. Someone was in it. Someone was in it and Michael was telling them where to — put their burden down. It was the river, moving faster, and now — almost frozen. Just in time they reached the edge. Heave ho, Michael said, heave ho, they all said, and they threw the black box in. It was just in time, the water . . . wasn't quite frozen. Someone screamed. It was Frances . . . Frances — and Michael was alive. She tried to wake, but dream stuck to her feet like mud from the bottom of the pond. She was frozen there, mud was frozen. Caitlin cried from far away. Coming closer, a procession — taking Michael to the river — No — bringing Michael back, with — Caitlin in his place — Caitlin in his place in the water. Michael dropped her in the water there to die.

23

"Just spend as much time with Katherine as you need," Alan said. "I'll take care of Caitlin." Yesterday Fran had come home escorted by two elderly strangers. Covered with a blanket, she clutched the baby. Her jeans were wet to the knees. Nothing — not the nightmares, not her strange behavior after Cait's birth — nothing until now has made him feel she was in danger, or seriously unbalanced. A crisis! When he had been sure that her treatment must almost be over. It was still not possible to *feel* the danger. It was like the time his dad had an accident with the power saw. "Run get your grandma," he'd said. And Alan felt nothing, nothing at all, and ran and was able to say — as if telling Nona to go out and buy more nails — "Call the ambulance, Dad cut off his finger."

He didn't have to look at the clock to know it was time to heat Caitlin's bottle. She should be weaned to a cup soon, he knew. That's what her three grandmothers said, at any rate. And he would be the one to like that most — not just for the end of night feedings, but because he liked things done at the appointed time. Today he would have to mail two more queries to *Parents Magazine* and *Newborn Gazette*. Without ten story ideas in the mail at any time, he felt exposed — which probably saved his freelancing ass. They had a reasonably steady income. But how much was enough if you struck out on your own? Struck out — a good choice of words — a man could go down — three strikes and you're out. He could never answer budget questions with numbers — something else always intervened: images from that last summer in their old house before they moved in with Nona — his father sitting at the kitchen table all morning with a newspaper, his mother whispering to someone on the phone, and nine year old Alan in the corner building a rusty bridge with his erector set over a bump in the linoleum.

An experimental whimper from Caitlin. He was glad because he didn't feel like working and she gave him an excuse. Perhaps they should drive over to Nona's this morning and stay for lunch.

But when Nona opened the door as far as the chain, she acted as if she expected to close it again, fast, upon a magazine salesman. "Oh, Alan, it's not a good time for you to bring the baby. Your mother has another migraine, and I was just going to bring her a compress."

"Where's Dad?" Alan said, and was immediately surprised at himself. He never came to see his father. His dad had mellowed out in recent years, but he didn't have a lot to say to him.

"Oh, don't you remember — he's been working for Larry's Auto back of the Wimpys on Central. Every Saturday. Some people shouldn't retire. I told him."

His feet took him toward the garage where he found his dad bent over the engine of a '69 Cougar. A mechanic, who looked barely out of high-school, kept pushing a forelock back from his eyes as he peered intently at two wires held by the older man. "*First* you check to make sure there's a goddamn connection," his father said, but not unkindly. He gave the boy a cuff on the arm and turned to the door.

"Well Alan, and my favorite granddaughter." He started to wipe his hands on a rag hanging from the back pocket of his coveralls and then seemed to think better of it. "Back in a minute," he said.

Alan looked around the garage. Like every garage his father had ever worked in — this one was clean. The vise grips were arranged according to size, the cable was coiled on the wall, and no oil was puddled under cars for long. When he was a boy it was his job to put down the industrial absorbent sawdust, sweep it up, and scour the cement-embedded stain.

"How about going over to Bruno's for a hamburger and beer," his father said, a little tentatively, "or did you have some business here . . . ?"

Alan shook his head. "Nona said you were free around noon. Okay with Larry if you go early?"

"Larry!" His father kicked aside a ramp guide, then stooped over, put it carefully upon two wall hooks. "Larry wouldn't know his ass from a hole in the ground, even if he was here. He leaves it all to me Saturdays."

His father didn't like to talk when he ate, so Alan drank his beer in silence. The hamburger, scorched on the outside and raw in the middle, made a lump in his stomach. He wondered why he had come. A fine provider he was — leaving his desk after one hour's work — no matter that it was Saturday. His dad never took the whole weekend off until retirement, and that lasted only two months. And look at him now — funny that he didn't choose to work on a weekday.

Caitlin, sucking on a dill pickle, was making comical faces. The men laughed. She's a useful topic of conversation, thought Alan. She sneezed.

"Getting a cold?" asked her grandfather, as he dabbed at her nose and chin with a napkin.

"I hope not," said Alan. "Her buggy rolled a little ways into North Lake yesterday, but I don't think she got wet at all, just Fran, getting her out."

"What? In this weather! Women. That's the sort of dumb thing your mother would have done — paying no attention while she gabbed with some biddy."

Alan felt his ears get hot — like a teenager. If he'd been that boy in the shop, he would have punched Leo back. "Fran's very careful with her; it was a freak accident." His tone was even, but inside he felt . . . like he hadn't felt in years. He'd been proud that he'd grown to accept his parents the way they were. He'd never been able to understand why Fran had a problem with her mother. "Well, I better think about getting back, Dad."

"What's the hurry? You're self-employed, though I don't know if being without a steady paycheck — you know, something you can count on each month, is a good idea for a family man." Leo looked over at the bartender. "Bring us another one, Bruno." He smiled at Alan, gaps showing either side of his eyeteeth. Alan looked at, not in, his father's eyes — the rims of white showing below each iris. As a boy he thought no one else had eyes like that. He thought that his father's eyes were like that because of the pressure in his head when he got mad. Pop-eye, but not exactly. Not funny.

"Just a half," Alan said.

"You're self-employed, son, but that also means you're wife-employed. Gotta watch out for those women. Never caught me with the dirty diapers on my day off. Gotta watch those women." Leo took a long drink of beer, reached for some peanuts.

Why, he thinks we're having a man to man talk, Alan thought; he doesn't mean any harm.

"You've got to show a woman who's in charge. Now I don't mean roughing her up, though some do. I never . . ."

"You never hit mom, you didn't have to, but you hit me." After little Alan came home from the hospital with a patch on his eye, Leo started wearing suspenders, which just snapped. And stung. "You hit me until I was almost eleven and then you stopped, but I remember."

His father, who was reaching for some more peanuts, tipped the bowl over. "Oops," he said, "Let me get that. I'll get us some more."

"No more beer for me," Alan said. Was his dad going to pretend he didn't hear him?

He watched his dad walk to the men's room. The old man's back swayed forward with the weight of his gut. And his head was tucked between his shoulders. When he came back, he didn't have another beer, and he hesitated before pulling out his chair. When he sat down, he went on looking at a spot just to the left of Alan's head.

"When you were little, I had a lot of problems. But we had some good times together too. It wasn't all Cub Scouts, stuff like that

89

doesn't bring a father and son together like real life problems. Do you remember how you ran to get help when I cut off my little finger to the first joint? You were cool in an emergency, and you got that from me. You might not remember the time at Sears Automotive, across the street from our house on Bryan, when you came over with a sandwich for my lunch and got to watching that young jerk, forget his name, take a car down with the hoist too fast. Well it slipped, and if I hadn't thought fast, if I hadn't pushed you back, you would've been crushed. I tell you all this so you know. And then the foreman came over and started yelling at me for letting you come into the shop. So I yelled back, and one thing led to another and soon after that I decided to open up an auto repair and filling station of my own, with some money Nona lent us. Well, you know the rest." He looked at Alan for the first time. "It's not good for a man to owe his mother-in-law. Oh, she always treated me with respect, and I was grateful, but it's not good. I'm not telling you this to make excuses."

"I wondered," Alan said. "I wondered if you were sorry."

24

FRAN TOLD KATHERINE about her dreams. She said, "Michael left her there to die." She hesitated.

"Was that all?" Katherine asked.

"No. I pulled Caitlin out, white and frozen. I carried her inside and my mother began to cry. I felt very guilty and said, 'I should have told you right away — Cait isn't dead, but stunned with cold.' I had the strong feeling — mother can't go through this a second time."

Fran sat up straight — like a brave child, Katherine thought. She told Katherine, "It's as if I were the strong one." Fran looked at her, as if expecting praise.

"Why does Michael torment you so? Why did he direct the others to kill you? Why did he want Caitlin to die in his place?"

"Katherine. This is so dumb. We're talking about a four year old dead boy."

"Alive in 33 year old Frances. No, we're talking *to* an eight year old girl."

"Yes. After what happened yesterday, I feel like a child. An inexcusably incompetent child." She looked away, her jaw rigid, her chin jutting.

She's angry with me, Katherine thought, and still terrified. She had a strong impulse to comfort Fran, and then caught herself. She shouldn't ignore Fran's anger, after misusing her own anger twice now. She shouldn't make that mistake again. She'd been angry with Fran because she, Katherine, hadn't been able to keep her own child. That was the truth. It was a mistake to act out your own private drama with a patient. Out of nowhere came the words: *If you are going to make a mistake, make it a big one.* A mischievous voice. Then — *Half a mistake is worse than no mistake at all.* By God, she had forgotten what she learned thirty-five years ago in her training analysis: *You must be the "bad" parent. You must not "want" your patient to get well so much that you force her health. If you sacrifice your patient to your own need to be the "good parent," she might lose her chance to suffer the old disease, and to cure herself.*

"Yes," said Katherine, "You did behave like a child yesterday. But that sort of regression is very natural. You're getting stronger. As a matter of fact, I think you are strong enough to hear some straight talk. Frances! Didn't your father tell you death is a part of life? Didn't your mother tell you, in every way she knew, not to complain? Didn't she give you an example of real courage? Didn't they both suffer a loss, feel a pain, greater than you would ever know? It's your job now to accept death. I don't mean to be harsh, but you just have to face facts." She paused. Had she caught the right idiom? Had she gone too far? Not far enough?

Frances held her hand to her cheek — as if she'd been slapped. "Face facts, face facts! You sound like my mother! If she were here, I'd tell her: '*You* of course are everything and *I* am nothing. Didn't you see how I wanted to be just like you? If you were such a strong and perfect person, why did I have to take the blame so you could go on being strong?

" 'I overheard you say Michael was more charming, Michael always smiled and made people laugh, he was so funny. But poor serious Frances, she gets so cross. I hated him! And after he died, I knew what you were thinking: She wanted her brother to die. Why wasn't *she* the one to die?

" 'Oh, how could I say that to you, Mom! I love Caitlin so much I'd die for her. You came running to get me out of the apple orchard, and you were crying, and I cried and cried, and we both cried for Michael.

" 'But why didn't you ever speak of him again? I mean really talk — not, Michael is a little saint in heaven, Amen, but really talk? Because it hurt so much? Because you thought it would hurt us to see you hurt? Oh, mother it hurt more when you never cried again. We were so close. It was over, I wasn't allowed to feel bad. I thought I *was* bad.

" 'I'm not a bad person, I'm a person who feels very, very sad.' "
Fran put her head in Katherine's lap and began to cry.

25

A CATHARSIS WAS ALL very well and good, Katherine thought while she was getting ready for their session the next day, but she hoped Fran realized they still had unfinished business.

A needless worry. Before Fran even kicked off her loafers, and tucked her feet under her on the big chair, she said, "I've been thinking more about the dream of Caitlin in the icy water — how when I brought her in to my mother, I was the reassuring strong one and my mother was the weak one. Does that dream show that I wanted or want her weak, or myself strong? Or both?"

"What do you think?"

"I don't know. And something else bothers me. You asked me why Michael tormented me, why he wanted Caitlin to die in his place? And then you talked about eight year old Frances still living inside me. Did you mean that *I*, a part of me, was sacrificing my own child?"

"It's not what I meant, it's what you feel. Do *you*, in a part of yourself, feel you don't deserve to have a child?"

"Because I felt, or still feel, guilty? I couldn't believe it yesterday — when I remembered how I felt about Michael, I spoke like a child. Do you know — he was the *only* brother or sister I remember resenting!"

"You never let yourself be 'bad' again."

"Did I think I could kill them with my feelings? Did I think that somehow I killed Michael?"

Fran, now cross-legged in the chair, leaned toward her, and she was — spontaneous! When we first met, thought Katherine, Fran's direct speech seemed like candor. "If so, then you must have felt both responsible and powerful. Children aren't supposed to feel so powerful. It must have made you angry."

"Oh, despite feeling angry yesterday, I don't remember being angry then."

"At first you didn't remember that your mother became hysterical when she ran to find you in the apple orchard. It did you much good to remember how she cried."

"I think the dream means I see her and myself as both strong and weak. Somehow, the dream helped me remember how we cried together." Fran took a deep breath, put her thumb and little finger together, as if to hold her feeling long enough to turn it into words. After a few moments, she said, "So now it means more to think of

93

the times she showed courage. I remember when Mark broke his arm for the second time, she said it was better for him to wear a cast than avoid all risk. She said the most difficult task she had after Michael's death was not to cripple us with her fears.''

"It never occurred to her she could isolate you with her strength," said Katherine. She looked at her desk, and her chair behind it. How had she ever pictured her office as a professional fortress? She saw now that nothing could protect her from Fran, and she gave the right wheel of her chair a turn forward, which made her slightly awry. Fran pulled on the left to put her straight. How appropriate, thought Katherine.

"That's right! But now I feel more like her — I'm brave with Caitlin every day — even yesterday, when I was foolish. I haven't avoided risk." Fran sighed. "She told me how, after Michael died, she would move the ironing board around from window to window, so she could watch us while she worked. We never knew."

As Katherine listened, she doodled a walled city — first use of the note pad lying idle on her lap. In the center was a tower — foursquare. She ringed it with a moat. As she had wished to do — in some ideal analytical objectivity – she smiled and rejoiced at Fran's insights. Then she said, "I'd like to tell you something about myself. I'm not so sure why I didn't tell you sooner. It would have helped you understand why I became angry with you. But then you might have misread everything else I had to say – thinking it was more about me than you. . ."

"Good grief, Katherine, tell me!"

So. She had to tell Fran about Emma: "I can understand and admire your mother, Fran." No hidden watching at the window for Katherine, once her own night watch was over. No good reason for her silence. "I used to say what happened to my child was crib death, or sudden infant death syndrome, and putting on those labels was, like the few things your mother said about Michael, a way of thinking that hurt less – giving death a name." Then Katherine heard herself, as if she were someone else, talk about the small things too: "It happened in her sleep; I'd always heard her until that night. Even when uncomfortable, she made a little chuckling sound in her throat, when she saw me. She had humor, she smiled when she grabbed a strand of my hair as I bent over her." Fran looked stricken, but Katherine continued anyway. "That was 32 years ago," she said, "and it's more painful now than it has been in two decades. Because of you. How could I tell you these things without hurting you? But pain is not such a bad thing. So why not tell you sooner? Because I wanted you to come to know your mother. I wanted you to identify with your mother, not with me.''

94

"Why couldn't I identify with both of you?"

"Now you can. Before, I don't think so . . . Fran, I didn't have another child. From choice. I made a choice out of fear. You said you would never give God a second chance to take a child of yours. That's the way it was with me."

Fran crossed her arms on her chest and looked down. When she didn't say anything, Katherine asked, abruptly, "Was your mother angry?"

"About Michael? If she was, she never said." Fran frowned. "I just remembered something. She told me that Dad had her come along in the ambulance to the hospital, even though Michael was already dead. She said for a long time she didn't know why he thought it would help her to see his body."

With some effort, Katherine lifted her thigh — just a fraction of an inch. She looked down at her flaccid left arm. Emma's body. The perfect, rounded limbs, sculptured features. The rib cage of a child — so light, a fragile chrysalis. At a glance, you know the child doesn't live there any more.

"It helps — eventually — to have seen your child. Your father was right." Katherine was close enough to Fran to compel her, but Fran had gone off somewhere. Katherine gripped Fran's arm with her one good hand. "So your mother wasn't angry. But you were very, very angry. You still are. And how do you know your mother wasn't angry? I was. Angry and afraid." She pointed to her metal file cabinet. "After Emma died I bought that. In case the house burned down in the night. So I wouldn't lose my manuscripts too."

There — the analyst's done it again — told the patient what to feel! But she, from the expression on her face, wasn't following instructions. The patient was deeply sorry for the analyst, who didn't know if she could handle that. Humbug! Katherine told herself, when Fran embraced her, you *need* this! Fran had plenty of time to learn how to be angry.

26

ALMOST AS SOON AS Caitlin's birth, Alan's grandmother and Fran's mother had begun pestering them about the baptism. Nona made solemn references to Limbo: "Of course nothing will probably happen, but with all the flu going around and this new SIDS they talk about, you shouldn't take any chances." Alan was furious with her, although she hadn't been told of Fran's fears. Fran's mother grew increasingly uneasy about Caitlin's age — "If you wait much longer, Cait will be walking to her own baptism." — as if some essential order had been broken. "They seem to think a baptism is magical," Fran commented to Alan. His mother didn't say a word, but she looked at Fran as if she had, somehow, guessed at something wrong — something more than the baby blues.

Then, just a few weeks after the scare at the pool, Fran said she was ready to have Caitlin, now nine months old, baptized. It would be in the small church in Fisherton near the lake cottage, Fran decided. "Let us know," her father said. "We'll come any time before the snow flies." It was only an hour from the Twin Cities, Alan told his father, when he objected to the distance. "Come on, you go four hours to Itasca for hunting!"

Alan wanted Fran to do the driving when they went to Fisherton, but Fran had allowed her driver's license to lapse. He thought her isolation at home with the baby was unhealthy, and decided it would push her a little to set a date for her "coming out." He decided not to check in with Katherine. If this didn't fit with the course of Fran's analysis, Fran could tell him herself.

He said, "It's important to you. It's important to me."

"*I* know I'm better," Fran said, "but the *dreams* don't know just yet." She still had nightmares of putting her foot to the gas pedal, and not being able to raise it: Her foot was attached to the floor — a demonic adhesiveness resulting in uncontrollable speed. She said the car dreams reminded her of the dream of wind, curtains clinging to her hands.

It came back to him what his driver's license had meant when he was sixteen. "My dad said, 'Think you're pretty big, now? Well, you're still a little punk. The first time you get a ticket, the first time you come home late, you'll never see these keys again.' " Now, no time to guess what she needed to hear. He only knew what he needed to say. He took Fran's hands and tugged them to emphasize his words.

"Fran, for me, driving was power, control. I was driving away from *them* — do you see?" She nodded. "It's even more important now, when we're driving, in a sense, *toward* them."

That night Fran dreamed she tried to wrench her key from the ignition to stop her wildly careening car. The following night, when she was once again traveling at an unwilled velocity, she was able to lift the pedal up, lower her left foot onto the clutch, and in one easy motion, shift back into third, then second, then first. She slowly brought the car to rest. The next week she retook her driver's test and passed.

All of Fran's Minnesota-based family went to Fisherton for the baptism. Cress was there, and their youngest sister, Jenny. Mark came from Michigan. As for Alan's family — he was amused to see that his mother, with an air of understanding complicity, gave Fran a car seat for the baby. "She's too big now, for the Snugli, isn't she?" she said. Alan was pleased to see his father's new sports jacket. Leo called himself grandpa, and as soon as Fran, Alan and Katherine arrived, he put out his arms for Caitlin.

Something about a man holding a baby. A choice. The man reaches out. Or doesn't. Or just watches the way the woman and her child are close together, blown together. Or apart. And doesn't know his role in all of that. After a while his father didn't lay a hand on him again. Not at confirmation. Not at graduation. At six he had pretended he couldn't ride his two wheel bike, so his dad would start him off with one tight hug and a gentle push on the back. When he was sixteen, his father said, "You'd better go to Driver's Ed — where they don't know you like I do."

What he had liked best about driving, when he was a teenager, was the way the whipped air filled their old Chevy, through the open windows, and sometimes, when he topped seventy, it seemed the wind might take the roof off, and he felt so free that anything — even a highway cop, even a boot from his father — was worth that rush. What would my father say if I told him the wind has a penis, Alan wondered, if I just went up to him and said, Dad, there's something I want you to read. It's by this guy called Jung. Then I'd pull out this creased piece of paper I've been carrying in my pocket . . . no, I have it by heart, I'd say. Listen, Dad, you and I — we're a lot more important than we thought. Listen:

There's this erect prick on the disc of the sun. And that's where the wind come from. He'd say, you're not supposed to drink before a baptism. And if I told him this was a vision from one of Jung's schizophrenic patients, would he say I was crazy too? Would I go on and say, No, Dad, Listen: This crazy man said, when he moved his head from side to side, the sun's penis moved with it. That's power

Dad, I'd say — "crazy men like us want power. Our pricks are the origin of the ministering winds! Then he'd say, that's no kind of language to use outside a church. He'd say, there's only one kind of wind around here — and it's blowing fore and aft. Okay, dad, I'd say, break wind with me! Then could I tell him the best part? The wind fertilizes and creates! Jung, Amen. Or would he run away?

Alan went back to his father and held out his arms to the baby. Leo hesitated, put his cheek on hers. She bounced forward, kicking at her white wool baptismal dress. "We have to have another talk real soon, Dad."

"We will," his father said, and handed him the baby. Then he looked away, pulling at the neck of his shirt, loosening the knot of his tie. He opened the door of the church and stood aside for Alan and the baby.

The priest helped Fran and Alan renounce the devil for Caitlin. Fran held a lighted candle, and Alan covered her with a long white cloth. Caitlin cried when the water trickled into the fat creases of her neck, into the corners of her eyes. After the priest had finished, and gone back into the sacristy to change, before he joined them at the cottage for dinner, Alan cleared his throat. "I have something I'd like to read — an addition to the ceremony." He felt very nervous — like someone who has finally acted out an obsessive fantasy of interrupting a church service. Then he felt very calm — it was, after all, his child. And this would be much easier than reading his fiction to strangers. He wanted to mark, to underline, the mysterious order of their lives. He looked at his mother, and Fran's mother, and read,

"That which is born of the flesh is flesh, and that which is born of the Spirit is spirit . . ."

He looked at Fran and continued,

"The wind blows where it will, and you hear the sound, but do not know its origin, nor its destination: so it is with everyone who is born of the Spirit."

"And this is especially for you, Katherine," he said. "It's from Jung:

"To be born of water simply means to be born of the mother's womb; to be born of the Spirit means to be born of the fructifying breath of the wind . . ."

Fran looked at him — the old eye shift, bulls-eye! — and he felt very close to her. Fran's mother came up behind her, circled her with her arms, and said to Alan, "I don't know what that means, but it sounded very good." His mother started to cry.

"Well done," said Katherine.

Alan noticed that his father and Nona were getting restless so he turned and lead them all out of church.

They lingered at the cottage until long after dark around the fireplace. Caitlin waved her hands at the flames until she fell asleep. Around an evening with family, Alan thought, we draw a magic circle. But he was drowsy too, so they stepped in front of the fire and went outside again. They were pulled by the freeway into sudden faceless headlights, boring into skulls, past hurtling metal shells. And by some miracle, they came home.

27

OVER IN THE CORNER Tillie Napsen had her hand in a strange rubber glove with sausage-like fingers. Bands stretched from each finger to her palm. She stared at her hand and moved one finger slowly, till the band tightened. "That's to keep her hand from forming a claw," the therapist explained to Katherine. "It's good for patients to keep trying, no matter what," she added. No matter if it didn't do any good? Katherine wondered. She looked away. How did Tillie, did anyone, stand it? Was senility an escape from the prison of the body? If so, Tillie was well out the door, into a hallway that led nowhere. Through the bars and pulleys of P.T., Katherine could see the north corridor of 1-C, repeating itself forever, dead-end doors at regular intervals — as unconvincing as multiple images in a mirror.

"Let's work on pelvic position today," the physical therapist said. And so they began again: "Now when you feel me push your hip to the right, you push back to the left." After only fifteen minutes, Katherine felt beads of perspiration on her forehead. Tired before she'd begun?

Then, from the corner of her eye, she saw Fran come through the door. At the sight of Fran, Katherine didn't want to continue. She wanted to say, "Let Fran take me home now; I don't feel well today."

Fran looked up at the clock. "Oh, I'm really early, aren't I! Caitlin threw me off by eating so fast." Katherine smiled and started to speak, then stopped. If I ask her to take me home, Katherine thought, she'll think it's because I don't want to waste her time and she'll feel bad about coming early. Well, only forty-five minutes to go.

The therapist, seeming to pick up Katherine's resistance, said, "Why don't we take a break for a few minutes?"

"What is the purpose of your holding her hip in that position?" Fran asked.

Katherine wanted to laugh but she felt too weak. The therapist had hardly been "holding" her; on the contrary, what appeared to be so static was actually a sort of therapeutic contest between herself and her therapist. But that was hard to explain. So she was glad when the therapist said, "This is a type of patterning. It's supposed to reawaken the connection between the nervous system and the muscles. The old idea used to be strengthening the individual muscles — lifting weights etc. An even older approach was to allow the stricken side of a stroke patient to atrophy, while strengthening the good side to take over all movement."

"This is certainly a more optimistic method," Fran commented. "You're not going to let Katherine leave her bad side behind, even if she sometimes would like nothing better."

She means that for herself too, Katherine thought. Fran smiled at her with full meaning — holding every nuance in her eyes like a fanned deck of cards. When I first knew her, Katherine remembered, she selected what she knew, and it was a narrow choice.

"I have something to do with it," Katherine said. "Every time she pushes against me, I'm supposed to return the pressure. It may look like nothing much is happening to you, but yesterday I moved her hand back a good quarter inch! This is work!"

Fran grinned. "Force, counter-force. You even have to fight your own therapist to improve."

Katherine laughed, and felt happy for the first time that afternoon, but still a little shaky too. She thought it might be her blood sugar, so she ate a small slice of cheese and drank some orange juice. Then they went back to work. But after only five more minutes, her back felt oily with sweat. When she tried to swallow, her throat felt tight. Then it was difficult to breathe.

The therapist quietly took her pulse. She frowned, and then smoothed out her expression — the required blandness, Katherine thought with apprehension. "Now, this is probably nothing but fatigue, but I'm going to see if the doctor is still in O.T. Just to be on the safe side, I'd like him to see you." She looked at Fran, who, Katherine noticed, was standing very still.

As the doctor drew the curtains around the hospital bed in the corner, Katherine thought, Oh, God, no, I hate these beds. Then the cold flat disk of the stethoscope on her breast. A nurse padding in to draw blood. A technician wheeling in the EKG machine, clackety, clank. Once again strapped and diagrammed. It seemed she could see the pages of her chart blowing off into the future like leaves off a calendar tree.

But the doctor was only hearty. No sentence this time. He delivered a warning, secondhand, through the therapist. "Now just a half hour for Katherine tomorrow, and I'll check her after the session. If there's any difficulty, maybe she should only come in every other day." He turned to Fran. "I've written another blood pressure prescription for her." Then he seemed to recall that Katherine was still there. He bent over her and said something that made her heart skip: "You have to think about maintaining what you've gained."

28

"I'LL FEEL MORE LIKE talking when we get home," Katherine said. So Fran drove in silence, and glanced at her sidewise as she shifted. It seemed to Katherine that St. Clothilde's loomed behind them, as if defying all laws of perspective, growing larger as they drove away from it. She had prickles on the back of her neck.

When they pulled into the driveway, she saw the light at the kitchen window switch on. Dusk, this indeterminate time of day, Katherine thought, when it is still light outside, but growing too dim inside. The time when burglars watch houses. If no lights go on, bad luck for the householder. Was a burglar, even now, skulking away from them through the shrubbery? Up until now, her house had been safe. Someone had always been home . . .

As usual, Fran took the wheelchair down the ramp at the back, and then moved it around to the side door. But Katherine was fumbling for her four-pronged quad cane.

"Katherine, do you think you ought to exert yourself?"

"I'm not dead yet," Katherine said. Winter would stop her soon enough, she thought as she inched her way around so her legs were hanging out the side door. Then she held the back of the seat with her good hand, and pushed off, sliding down, to balance on her good leg. She released the seat, and reached again for her cane, but Fran was there before her and put the cane into her hand as she held the door open.

Katherine looked at her, for the first time since they left St. Clothilde's. "Aren't you supposed to let me be self-sufficient?" She tried to stride forward, her good leg and cane together, but her left leg dragged a little. She hitched up her right hip, willing the muscles to do their double work, but the left leg felt like — like nothing, like a wooden prosthesis, as bad as the early days. Finally, sweat running down either side of her nose, she swung her bad leg through. "I can manage, Fran."

She could feel Fran's eyes between her shoulder blades as she planted the cane ahead of her, and then, slowly, the heavy leg, heel first. Once she'd told Fran how hard it was for her to keep people waiting, how she'd noticed that even good friends were awkward when she approached a door: very hearty, joking, calling out greetings. "Well, I can see how you might worry about being slow when you've never been slow before, but as for other people," Fran had said, "I think they — I know I — admire how mobile you have become since your stroke." But Katherine had shaken her head. "Maybe so, but if I stuttered, half the people I meet would not be able to restrain themselves from finishing my sentences. I guess I should be thankful that no one else can try to walk for me."

It seemed to take a longer time than usual to negotiate the path to the door. Katherine was glad that other people — Fran especially — couldn't read her thoughts. She didn't want anyone else to know how little surprised she really was by her angina — if that was what it was. For months now it had been — a little twinge here, a tiny pain there. Like you tell your patients, Dr. Morgan, she scolded herself, if you ignore your feelings you'll develop a nice little neurosis, or an aneurism, just to get your own attention. Or whatever. She might have seen the mechanism in her own case . . . if she hadn't been distracting herself with "family" matters, that is. . .

Just as Katherine reached the ground level front door, Fran stepped ahead of her to hold the door for her stiff-legged swing over the sill. Then she steered Katherine quickly to the right, and Katherine only scraped the molding on the left. "Should have let me knock my silly self out," Katherine muttered.

Alan was in the kitchen making spaghetti, singing a medley of old James Taylor songs, banging the colander on the sink, running water on the pasta.

"Come on in the living room," Fran called. "Katherine and I could sure use a glass of wine before dinner."

The familiar clutter of Alan's chess pieces and manuscripts, Caitlin's stuffed animals, Fran's magazines and coffee cups, her own book on the corner table where she'd left it only yesterday. This family hodgepodge, that wasn't hers to order, only hers to enjoy — like a long ago memory of visits in her cousins' homes.

"Chilled white Zinfandel coming up," said Alan. Katherine's hand shook a little when he handed her a glass. "What's wrong," he asked. "Did you two have a fight?"

"No," Fran said, "She used to get me to fight with her, but now I'm cured."

Katherine thought, good, let Fran do the interpreting in this relationship for once. She sipped her wine and remembered the night they'd driven home from the baptism. No one had much to say. Katherine watched the back of Fran's head, the confident way she moved her head from side to side along the road. "You have to be careful — it's so easy to start looking in one direction and then go into a trance when you're driving. That's how many accidents happen," Fran had said, "especially at night." Katherine had watched Alan, too — the way he

103

kept reaching over to stroke Fran's thigh. They've forgotten I'm back here, Katherine thought. She'd tried to match her breath to the baby's sleep-breathing. They had even forgotten Caitlin. Well, a job well done, Katherine had told herself.

"Katherine?" said Alan. "Are you all right? I asked if you wanted any more wine?"

Katherine nodded.

"Are you depressed about the therapy being cut back?" Fran asked, and Katherine felt confused. Fran's therapy? Weren't they finished with that? Then she realized that Fran had been referring to her weak spell at St. Clothilde's. Driving home after the baptism, Katherine knew that Fran was no longer her task, and she thought, what do I think about now? My heartburn? What if it's not heartburn? And it wasn't.

"Katherine had an upsetting talk with the doctor," Fran said. Katherine took a sip of her wine, another, and let her breath out until it was safe to speak. "I hadn't ever expected to walk without a cane again, but I did think . . . He didn't spell it out, but he's concerned about my blood pressure. Despite the pills. I hadn't actually faced the possibility of another, more severe, stroke . . ."

It was a funny feeling. Like strengthening your back muscles after you fall off a ladder, only to discover that the exercise has aggravated your arthritis, like being in a train wreck after missing the airplane disaster, like being saved from drowning only to expire of pneumonia — like nothing she'd ever felt before, or had she?

That flat feeling. She had to ask Alan some day — was it something like that when a writer finished a story? There sat Fran and Alan, in control of their own chapter. Fran looked — solid. Realized.

And why should her own poor health make such a difference now? Why now, when, after all, her stroke brought them together in the first place? No, all Katherine knew was — she had been going somewhere and all of sudden she wasn't. And in some way she didn't understand yet, her fixed reference point, her "home," was altered too.

"But neurodevelopmental therapy seems so gentle," Fran said, and then fell silent.

As if changing the subject, Katherine looked around the room at Fran's paintings. All the work of the past eighteen months, overflowing into the hall and dining room. Fran's earlier grids had gradually given way to a less confined composition — still a severe geometry, yet one part of a painting tugged at another part, seemingly one brushstroke away from dissolution, flying apart from the center, yet held together by some mysterious gravity. And next the introduction of minute connections, like threads, then hinges, then bridges. In the latest painting, a luminous pulsating cloud, or amnion, too formless to be womb, and out of it — some joyful kicking.

"These are very impressive, Fran. Like many promising young artists, you need more exposure. Perhaps you have thought, sometime, of going to New York, to try the galleries there?"

Fran's face was blank, and she shrugged. As Katherine knew very well, she hadn't made much of an effort yet with the dealers in the Twin Cities.

"Fran needs to pay more attention to the business end of her art," Alan said, "but we'd better go in and have dinner before Caitlin wakes up."

The spaghetti was delicious — Nona's recipe with olive oil and eggplant. It stuck in Katherine's throat. She knew that Fran and Alan had been saving her feelings when they ate together — with stir-fries, the thin meat pre-sliced, with stews and pastas. She knew, though it was done off-stage, she still needed someone to cut her meat. She put her fork down.

"Yes, I think we should talk about our situation, Fran. This living arrangement isn't fair to you and Alan. Maybe you'd like to get another job that would give you some wider experience. I'll be permanently disabled. I have to face it, and so do you. It's not right for us to continue, when I thought this would be temporary. . ."

"You thought . . . a temporary arrangement! Are you firing us? Should I pay you, then, for our sessions?" Fran got up and went over to her latest picture, hesitated, and said, "No, something's still coming out of this one." She picked the green one, mushroom shapes spearing each other as they multiplied. She set it down with a clunk at Katherine's feet.

When Alan didn't say anything, Katherine knew she had to continue. "Fran, don't misinterpret. We have a life connection — no matter where we go. It's time you had a home of your own." Still Alan didn't say anything, and she knew she was right. "Mitzi has been talking about going into practice with me," she lied. Or there would be plenty of practice at St. Clothilde's. But that didn't bear thinking of.

"And you need our side of the duplex?" Alan asked. She knew he almost believed her.

One cure between the two of them, and wasn't it right that it was Fran's?

Fran looked at her, hard. "What are you up to? Are you giving up?" Katherine shook her head, no, but was she? And didn't people lie to their nearest and dearest all the time? Could she really keep Fran and Alan on the periphery of her life like her "sister," Peggy — who was one lie she'd leave in place — to protect them from being her next of kin? She didn't know what she was going to do, and that was the truth. But Alan had to think what he needed to think, and Fran could guess what she wished.

"You're too damn stoic!" said Fran. "You're just like my mother!" Her cheeks were pink. She was still angry. "The whole rest of your life is temporary," she added. "So is Cait's life, and she's only nine months old." The last word, but it didn't change anything — temporary. Maybe that was good enough.

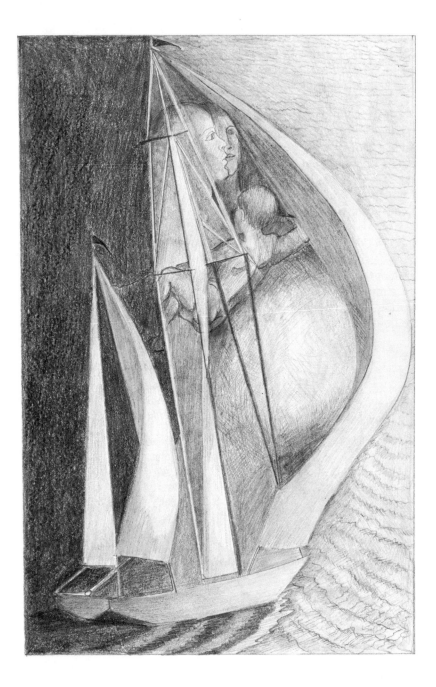

29

AT THE THAW-END of winter, Fran was pregnant again. "Katherine, she said, "don't you see? I need to keep my present employment."

Katherine didn't say yes, and didn't say no. Her illness had put her in a state of productive timelessness — living, not unhappily, from day to day.

Then Fran brought her a dream — as a present, to say thank you:

Alan, Frances and the baby are traveling at immense speed toward home in a sailboat. Down the length of the hull is a long harp-shaped wooden shuttle. The sail moves up and down the shuttle, from stem to stern, to catch the wind and hold it, steady. Fran is heavy, is ballast, speeding toward the shore, the lighted windows where . . . her mother moves, ironing clothes. Outside, the playing children . . . do not know their mother . . . follows them. Her silence is — gift. Streetlights on, Frances. . . will fly home free.

Photo: Stan Barone

Biographical Notes

Patricia Barone says of her background that "storytelling was and is a family pastime; my mother is Irish, my father is German, and they have competing family mythologies." She has studied painting and printmaking (disciplines which make such a large contribution to *The Wind*) and has taught art and religion. For six years she was a media coordinator for a private school in New Orleans, where she met her husband Stan. For the past nine years—since the birth of their two children—she has made her home in Fridley, Minnesota, a stone's throw from the Mississippi. She began her writing career as a poet but has, more recently, concentrated on fiction. *The Wind* began as a poem, became a short story, and finally a novella. It is Ms. Barone's first book.